Run for Your Sweet Life

RUN FOR YOUR SWEET LIFE

BY REX BENEDICT
PICTURES BY DAVID CHRISTIANA

FARRAR, STRAUS AND GIROUX

NEW YORK →

For Trub, who ran good

Run for Your Sweet Life

There was trouble on the border, and Awful Ivan Hoffenhoff was just the man to handle it.

"With me in charge," he announced, "folks can sleep sounder in their beds at night."

With him in charge, you didn't dare *get in* your bed at night. A shambles always followed when Constable Ivan Hoffenhoff took charge.

It was dangerous to be near him. Any suspicious movement—real or imagined—sent him into furious activity. Take, for instance, those mysterious and suspicious movements along the border. He was always tangled up in some bush he had pounced on, thinking it had moved. "Phantoms," he whispered when this happened. Now you saw them. Now you didn't. Made it awfully hard to pounce successfully. On the wings of his imagination, which was truly a wonder to behold, Awful Ivan fancied these border phantoms as swarms of alien intruders, some visible, some invisible, all of them with painted faces and some with knives between their teeth.

In his wild imaginings, the painted faces turned into painted bodies, then dancing bodies, then shrieking bodies, and then goodness knows what kind of bodies. The knives became stilettos, then daggers, then daggers with jagged edges, or machetes, then ancient swords that glittered in the dark, and poisoned, when they struck, the unlucky victim. And so on, and so on, with no end in sight. So that what in the beginning had been only swarms of alien intruders soon became, in his disordered mind, hordes of crazy Zacotans. Taking no chances, Awful Ivan called in his sub-constable, Halfway Hebe, and alerted the entire countryside to its peril.

Actually, with Awful Ivan in command, the countryside was already in peril. It was also on permanent alert, since Ivan put on an alert every other day and never bothered to take one off. He had put on an alert for flying saucers from the planet Hortex, which no one had ever heard of, and an alert for the Hortexians themselves, about which even less was known. "They're terrible," Ivan said, sparing his listeners the horrid details. They had to take his word for it.

And if the Hortexians were terrible, the Vortexians were

worse. Ivan had once surprised these strange creatures at some suspicious ceremony in the hills. Of course he had pounced. But since, as he explained it, they had repelled his pounce with some kind of force field, and overpowered him with odorless gas, and drugged him, and maybe hypnotized him too, he could hardly be expected to remember what they looked like.

Down but not out, Ivan plunged onward . . . upward . . . outward. Hortexians, Vortexians, Zacotans. "It's an invasion," he cried. "They're coming out of the bushes."

And just who—people wondered aloud—were the Zacotans?

Ivan's answer was to point ominously in the direction of what he called "Darkest Mexico."

To give Ivan credit, something *was* coming out of the bushes. The fact that he couldn't see clearly may have been due to his poor eyesight. Or it may have been that the intruders were taking great care not to be seen. Making matters even more one-sided, Awful Ivan himself was easy to see. In fact, you couldn't miss him. He looked exactly like a huge circus bear, without, of course, the chain around his neck. No bush was big enough to hide him. As for Halfway Hebe, he looked just like Awful Ivan, only bigger. The intruders had no trouble concealing themselves. They came always by night, sometimes on foot, at other times in slow-moving trucks with no lights. They came cautiously, moving in and out of the bushes in their attempt to cross the Rio Grande. Once on the other side, they wasted no time heading north.

And so now, putting out one more alert, just in case, and stuffing *The Guerrilla Warfare Manual* in his pocket, Awful Ivan gathered up a few old firearms, an assortment

of clubs, and a pack of hungry Afghans to serve as blood-hounds. Then he piled everything except the dogs on the shoulders of Halfway Hebe and set out from Blessed Hacienda border station.

"March!" Ivan ordered Hebe and the dogs.

They hadn't far to go. Blessed Hacienda border station was almost on the river, when the river was dry. When the river was up, Blessed Hacienda was in the river. Right now, in midsummer, the river had very little water.

"Okay," Awful Ivan said, when they were settled in the mud, "let's see what the manual says."

Awful Ivan was at his best when plotting strategy. No plan or ruse, however impossible, escaped his attention. What escaped his attention here was what the guerrilla manual said, since it was already too dark to read. That was something Ivan had trouble doing even in the brightest light. "Never mind," he said. "I've got most of it in my head. Pays to have a good memory. One thing's for sure. To carry out gorilla warfare, you've got to think like a gorilla and act like a gorilla."

"Sounds simple," Halfway Hebe said. "How do we start?"

"The first thing you do," Ivan said, "when lurking in the mud like this, is to engage in what's called gorilla breathing."

That caught Hebe's fancy. "How does a gorilla breathe?"

"Through the mouth, of course. Makes less noise."

Hebe tried it. "Comes right natural," he said, his mouth wide open.

"Watch out for mosquitoes," Ivan said. "You can choke to death on the big ones. Now," the great guerrilla fighter went on, "you're supposed to smear yourself with mud—sort of blend into the terrain."

Hebe started smearing. First he smeared himself, then he smeared the dogs. Awful Ivan rolled in the soft spots until he was covered, too. Between dogs and constables, you couldn't tell where one started and the other stopped.

"This is sure nice slime," Hebe said. "Smears real good. Stinks a little, though."

"Keep your voice down," Ivan said. "I think I hear something moving. It's behind those bushes over there."

"Smells a little like a sew—"

"Shhh," Ivan whispered.

By this time, Halfway Hebe had taken a mud bath. Even his ears were plugged. He couldn't hear a word Ivan was saying. And that was, if something of a blessing, a pity as well. For Awful Ivan needed all the help he could get right then. Something was moving, all right. And not only in the bushes. In fact, several things were moving, all at the same time. Mostly the movement seemed to come from somewhere across the stream. But there was another and different movement in the treetops over their heads. And still another—like a slow-moving truck—just over the river. Awful Ivan laid one ear to the ground and kept the other open to the sky. Hebe did the same thing.

"Don't hear a thing," Hebe grunted.

"Shut your muddy mouth!" Ivan said.

Now Ivan's "ground" ear was transmitting distant shuffling and scraping sounds, like bodies moving in the bushes and knives being whetted. "Hot dang!" he whispered. The "sky" ear transmitted even more ominous sounds, like the whir of motors approaching from the stars. "Saucers! The return of the Vortexians!" Ivan cried. Through muddy eyes he watched the Afghans. The sensitive beasts, he was certain, could sniff alien intruders anywhere this side of the moon. And sure enough their long noses were pointed directly up, then directly down, partly to the sky and partly to the other side of the stream, where the slow-moving-truck sounds came from. "They're coming from all sides," Awful Ivan cried. "Strange doings are afoot."

In truth, Awful Ivan Hoffenhoff and Halfway Hebe were crouched, mired in mud, in the middle of one of the strangest escapades ever recorded along the border. Ivan had probably invented stranger ones, but the difference was, this was for real. If there had been any doubt, it was soon removed. For in that moment of brushings, scrapings, whirs, and barking—the Afghans had set up a howl—a blinding flare shot out of the sky. Above the flare, plainly visible, a parachute drifted earthward. A man was clinging to it, and to what seemed a suitcase. When the flare touched down and died in the trees, the parachutist disappeared in blackness. Meanwhile, from the other side of the stream, the brushing and rumbling sounds could be heard coming closer.

Fearing for his life, Awful Ivan went into action. He shot to his feet, dripping mud, brandishing his clubs, pointing in all directions at once. The Afghans started leaping wildly at the prospect of a savage chase. "We'll meet them head-on!" Ivan cried.

The rumble grew louder. A vast black object came looming out of the darkness. Awful Ivan shouted, *"Lunge!"*

Through plugged ears, Halfway Hebe faintly heard, "Plunge!"

"Lunge!"

"Plunge!"

Actually, it scarcely mattered whether they lunged or plunged. They met nothing head-on, if you didn't count the truck which straddled them, and the water just deep enough to soften their fall. After that, they did little other than flop—to keep from being clubbed to death by Zacotans or eaten alive by Afghans.

2

No Afghan, however hungry, would have or could have eaten Awful Ivan Hoffenhoff alive. Or Halfway Hebe either. Nor were the two "gorillas" in any danger of being clubbed to death. The Zacotans, at least these Zacotans, did not carry clubs. As usual, Ivan's imagination had deceived him. His painted faces—could he have seen them—were nothing more frightening than the innocent faces of five dumb-struck kids. They had fallen from the rear door of the truck before it crossed the river. A bump had swung the doors open, spilled them out, and left them in the weeds. The

Dreamland Express, as the old Mack truck was called—with Gásparo the Coyote at the wheel—was supposed to deposit them in Blanco Canyon Hideout. Instead, it had deposited them in a ditch. Now, with the truck disappearing into the night, they huddled in the bushes, marveling at the sight of the two huge men and a pack of dogs flopping in the mud.

"What are they doin'?" asked one little guy.

"Looks like they're wrestlin'," was the reply.

"With dogs?"

"Everybody's all tangled up," another whispered. "I guess Gásparo ran over them."

"He's a pretty wild driver," said another.

"Yeah," whispered one of the very young voices. "When he hits you, you usually stay hit."

"It's certainly not a pretty sight," a girl's voice whispered.

These, then, were the dreadful Zacotans. One little girl, four little boys. Tiffany was the girl. She, like the boys, had chosen her new name with utmost care—in advance—to better fit her new life. Where she had got it, only Tiffany knew, though probably from American reruns on border television. She was about thirteen. The tallest boy, perhaps a little older, had easily assumed, and carried with style, the name of Slam Dunk Monte, another gift from television. Then came Marvin Lee, Dirty Little Harry, and finally Dirk the Turk. The last three were really little guys, around nine or ten years old. All the children's names—if you looked closely at them—told you clearly of their hopes and dreams, though right now it appeared they had few hopes and dreams. What they had most of all were fears, their greatest fear being the great glob of mud in the middle of the stream.

They had ceased to marvel at it and were busily trying to figure a way to get around it, or over it.

This was the first time in their many attempts to cross the border that the children had been separated from their parents. With a little luck, they might yet catch their families aboard the truck, which already the kids were calling the Gone-Forever Mack.

"How are we gonna get by those mud balls?" Slam Dunk Monte asked.

"We could walk on them," Marvin Lee whispered, "if they would stop moving."

"They look slippery to me," Dirty Little Harry whispered back. "Maybe if we just got up some speed, we could slide to the other side."

"And suppose the truck doesn't break down?" Tiffany asked.

"It always breaks down," Dirk the Turk whispered. "You can count on it."

"Tiffany's right," Slam Dunk said. "We could end up walking all the way to Blanco Canyon. That's over forty miles."

"We might die in the desert," Dirty Little Harry whispered. He made it sound rather glorious.

"Man, we're in trouble," Dirk the Turk said.

"Yeah," said Dirty Little Harry.

"Wait a minute," Slam Dunk whispered. "Maybe they're friendly. Let me get a closer look." He motioned for the others to keep down. Then he slid a little closer to the stream. Almost instantly, he came shooting back. "Unfriendly," he whispered. "Very unfriendly. It's the one they call the Pouncer!"

"You mean the one that's . . . " Tiffany tapped her head with her finger.

"That's the one," Slam Dunk whispered. "With his assistant. The one they call More So—because he's even worse."

"I thought they called him Halfway."

Slam Dunk waved his hand. "Halfway. More So. Whatever they call him, he's missing a wheel."

"I heard two wheels," Marvin Lee said.

It seemed that everybody on both sides of the border knew Awful Ivan and Halfway Hebe. Not wanting anything to do with them, the kids started scooting backwards. But scooting wasn't all that easy if you couldn't see where you were scooting. If you didn't scoot into a yucca plant, you scooted into a cactus, or something worse. Devil's-claws. Stickers. Burrs. Everything you bumped was sharp and vicious. It could tear you up pretty badly if your scootin' luck wasn't good, and theirs wasn't. In too big a hurry. A little frightened. Dirty Little Harry got jabbed badly, and Dirk the Turk was bleeding from two or three places, all of them very important ones for purposes of scooting. They would probably have scars to the end of their lives, which at the moment didn't seem very far away.

To complicate matters, somewhere someone must have sounded an alarm. And they must have sounded it all the way from El Paso to Brownsville. The entire border patrol seemed to arrive at once. Flashing their spotlights up and down the river, sirens screaming, they came in jeeps, panels, dune buggies, and motorbikes. It wouldn't have surprised the suffering little scooters if a squadron of tanks had pulled up and trained their guns on them.

"It's the *Migra!*" Slam Dunk said. "Led by the Great Migra

himself—Captain Mayhem. Now we're in worse trouble. Keep scootin', slow and easy."

"I think I'm bleedin' to death," Dirk the Turk said. The little turkey really was leaking badly. So were most of the others, except they were too busy scootin' to notice. They tried to keep their bodies hidden by the bushes. Even then, with the searchlights turning in all directions, they felt exposed. If they could just scoot out of sight before the thistles and the cactus did them in, they might have a chance.

The forces of the law had arrayed themselves on the other side of the river and were putting on a spectacular show. It was certainly worth watching, even at the risk of your life. The mangled scooters stared, fascinated, while scooting backwards inch by murderous inch. Now the assembled troops had scooped up Awful Ivan with a portable crane and deposited him and Hebe and the dogs on dry land.

"Pump the mud out of 'em!" roared Captain Girolamo K. Mayhem.

"That'll take some doing, sir," replied his aide.

"Are they legals or illegals?" Captain Mayhem asked, spreading out his maps and battle plans on a rickety card table.

"Don't look like either, sir."

"Whatta they look like?"

"Sponges, sir. Dirty sponges. Giant dirty sponges."

"Squeeze 'em and see if they drip."

The aide squeezed them. They dripped.

"They're sponges, all right."

Now the suffering scooters scooted less and less while watching more and more. No television movie had ever been as good as this. Dirty Little Harry actually started

scooting forward to get a better view—front row seat. Dirk the Turk forgot all about his recent punctures.

"Bring 'em up and stand 'em at attention," Captain Mayhem ordered. "We'll pass a few sentences."

"Dogs, too, sir?"

"Dogs, too."

"Best be careful, sir. I think the dogs are mean."

"So am I," Mayhem growled. "It'll be a fair fight."

With just the dogs to contend with, it might have been a fair fight. But that was to overlook Awful Ivan. No person in his right mind would do that. No person in his right mind *could* do that. Maybe Captain Girolamo K. Mayhem—as his troops had always suspected—was not in his right mind. Right or wrong, it was the only one he had.

"Put the cuffs on 'em," Mayhem roared, his great white mustache quivering at both ends.

"They don't make cuffs that big," the aide said. "I'll hobble 'em."

"Hobbles are extinct," the captain said.

"So are the suspects," the aide said, "to judge by their appearance."

By this time, Awful Ivan had recovered his wits. It always took him a while. Halfway Hebe had already recovered his, because he didn't have so far to go. Drawing himself up in all his muddy majesty, Awful Ivan thundered, "You spoiled the works! I had the Zacotans in a trap."

"You had who?" Captain Girolamo K. Mayhem thundered back.

Now that was a blunder on the captain's part. Smacked of ignorance. It was obvious that he had never heard of the Zacotans. Awful Ivan seized the opportunity to explain things. Inspiration overcame him. The more he talked, the more poetic he became, especially when he came to the part about the poisoned swords. Though Ivan had started out only with the Zacotans, his fancy soared effortlessly into realms unknown even to him. Among the names he dropped were those of the dreaded Mayacans, the fearful Aztecans, the wild Zapatans, Montezumacans, and finally the fierce Zobra Clan of the Zobracans.

"My God," the captain whispered, "so that's the way it is." The captain was impressed. Here was a man who had his head on right. He knew whereof he spoke. "What do you propose?" Captain Mayhem asked. It was obvious from his voice that he considered the situation a desperate one.

"Strike while the iron is hot," Awful Ivan said. "Call up reinforcements. The bushes are full of intruders. Hundreds of 'em just across the border. Right there!" He pointed directly at the spot where the children were watching the show. "They keep comin' night and day—mostly night."

"But that's foreign territory," Mayhem said. "You call it Mexico. Can't go bargin' in there. It's against regulations."

Awful Ivan drew himself up again, towering over everyone in sight. "You mean," he said scornfully, "you've never heard of the Hot Pursuit Law?"

Captain Mayhem braced himself for another shock. "Can't say that I have."

"Well," Ivan said, "let me give you the official version. It was just passed by various government bodies of various states, localities, municipalities, and townships. It says that if you're in hot pursuit of aliens from this or any other planet, you don't have to stop at the Rio Grande. Just plunge on, right on down to Guatemala if you like. I believe," Ivan himself plunged on, "it stipulates that you must stop only when you reach the Panama Canal, or somewhere thereabouts. By all means, do not go into South America. They have a severe epidemic of yak fever down there."

It little mattered to Awful Ivan that there were no yaks in South America. He was, as the saying goes, on a roll. Too bad he couldn't stay there. He might have inspired the captain and his forces to invade Mexico, and Guatemala, too. But the border was not a place that waited for speeches to end. Too many Zacotans and Zobracans about. Something was always happening.

What happened here was, Dirty Little Harry, leaning forward a bit too far to watch the show, fell into the river.

That brought the troops to their feet. "It's an ambush!" Mayhem cried. "Man the guns!"

Instantly, the night was alive with flashing lights, sirens, and barking dogs. Awful Ivan, of course, pounced, which direction it was hard to say, such was the confusion. Captain Mayhem knocked his card table over and fell on top of the battle plans, protecting them with his life. To protect himself, he ordered his troops to form a circle around him. One trooper cried out that he had been shot with a poison dart, and fancied himself paralyzed. Of them all, only Halfway Hebe maintained his calm. His ears still plugged with mud, he heard nothing, not even the jeep that almost ran him down in the mad scramble.

Across the river, Slam Dunk struggled frantically to lift Dirty Little Harry from the mud. That wasn't hard to do, since Little Harry had scarcely touched water before he started slithering back up the bank—on the run.

Running too, now, was Awful Ivan, followed by Halfway Hebe and the Afghans, straight for the river. "Defend the north bank!" Awful Ivan shouted to Captain Mayhem. "We'll flush 'em out."

"We'll hold the line," Mayhem roared back, "if it takes all summer."

"Run for your lives!" Slam Dunk cried.

It hadn't been necessary to tell them. All of them were already running for their lives. They were breaking every speed record, known or unknown. First they broke the sprint record, then the distance record, and were certainly on their way to breaking the marathon, if they didn't break their necks first. They were running at terrifying speeds, into what they hoped were the arms of safety—whatever that might turn out to be.

If you are running for your life, it is best to run into the arms of someone who is also running for his life. You might find sympathy. If you are fortunate enough to run into the arms of Suitcase Charlie Jones, you might actually find yourself thinking you had been saved. Certainly, Suitcase Charlie was qualified to save you. All his life he had been running for his life, was at the moment running for his life, and would probably be running for his life for the rest of his life.

So many people were pursuing him. On one side of the river, Captain Mayhem was pursuing him. On the other side, Captain Aguila García—known as the Eagle—was pursuing him. When not in hot pursuit of alien creatures, Awful Ivan was pursuing him. Even the tax collector was pursuing him. Charlie's activities, in their eyes, were suspicious, as were his connections. And it was true that Charlie had connections, the worst kind imaginable. They were pursuing him, too. Something to do with money. Charlie had a way of getting it mixed up. The Texas Connection and the Mexican Connection just couldn't figure out how he could fall out of an airplane with the wrong suitcase, which would be to say the one with the money in it.

But Charlie could do things like that. He did them easily, naturally, his way. When in trouble, he put his faith in his feet. Charlie was in the running game. Always had been. It was Charlie's feet against the world. He started young and never stopped. Runaway Charlie, they called him as a kid. Wrong-Way Charlie, they called him in school, when he got turned around and ran his most magnificent race in the wrong direction. Fast-Lane Charlie, they called him in the Army. *"That guy can run!"* his colonel cried, seeing Charlie streaming across the Asian terrain. "See how he floats. See how he streams. Never saw a guy run like that. It's beautiful!"

"It's his coordination, sir," the sergeant said, marveling also.

"Wrong!" the colonel said. "It's his dedication to his talent. He runs for love, life, the pursuit of happiness. He's daring the world to catch him." The colonel, mindful of the glory of the regiment, was already thinking, "Olympics!"

But Charlie was thinking otherwise. Streaming out of

the Asian brush—both feet intact—he dreamed of some more lofty goal. And besides, in the Olympics you had to run in the approved direction. Not Charlie's style at all.

Since Charlie's motives were pure, he assumed that good fortune was on his side. And it was, for a while. The newspaper ad had said simply:

WANTED
RUNNER
No Questions Asked
No Questions Answered

Pure freedom. A runner's dream. Charlie took the job. Suitcase Charlie, that was what they called him. Not until later did he find out that the "company" he worked for had no fixed address. And not until later yet did he find out what was in those suitcases he was "running." When he found out, his speed picked up considerably. Also, he began to run in circles. Soon—in the eyes of his beholders— he was doing suspicious things, the most suspicious of which was to leap from an airplane with what the Connection called the "loot."

Charlie hit the ground—as one would expect—running. Instinctively, he pointed his nose to the wind. That streamlined him. His nose was long and tapered, which cut down wind resistance. It occurred to him that he really ought to check his beard. Just a few matted hairs could badly damage the air flow. That was what he called "drag."

And there must have been some drag somewhere. Maybe it was the suitcase. For Charlie had just reached something approaching peak speed when the strangest thing happened. Someone passed him.

Then someone else.

Then another and still another.

And yet another.

"Heaven help me!" Charlie cried. "I'm in the loser's lane."

It did seem so. Nobody on this earth had ever passed Charlie Jones. Something was wrong, awfully wrong. Runners from outer space? They had seemed rather short for earthlings. Charlie speeded up. He relaxed every muscle. He blanked out all thoughts. He became the pure runner, floating, rising, falling, streaming, oblivious to the world around him. His attention to the world around him did not return until he floated past the five fleeing shadows. Swinging wide in an arc to avoid trampling anybody, he came round to meet them face to face. They stopped in their tracks, exhausted, gasping for breath, blowing air up at him.

"You've got us," one of them said.

"Yeah," said another, "we give up."

"Never give up," Charlie said. "True runners never give up." And then he added, "Keep running in place. Up and down. Up and down."

They could barely stand, much less run in place. Mostly they trembled in place.

"It's called winding down," Charlie went on.

They were already wound down.

"Up and down. Up and down," Charlie continued in a steady cadence. "Don't want any cramps. Where you headed?"

"Blanco Canyon." Dirk blew the words out in one big puff.

"You're goin' the wrong direction," Charlie said. "No big deal. I do it all the time."

"Right now, we're just goin' up and down," said Dirty Little Harry.

"We fell out of a truck," Marvin Lee said.

"And we survived," puffed Dirk the Turk.

"We hit hard," Dirty Little Harry said.

"And we bounced," Dirk said.

"How'd you get here?" Slam Dunk asked Charlie.

"Fell out of an airplane."

For some reason, that didn't seem to surprise them. Even in the dark, Charlie looked like the kind of guy who might fall out of an airplane. An airplane? A truck? It was all pretty much the same, except of course for the bouncing. No matter how you hit, you were in trouble.

Finally, Charlie called a halt to the winding down. The kids were relaxed now, though still short of breath. They looked at Charlie with curiosity.

"How come you're not breathin' hard," Marvin Lee asked, "like us?"

"And spittin'?" asked Dirty Little Harry. "Runners go around spittin' all the time."

Dirk the Turk and Little Harry were spittin' all over the place, while Charlie hadn't spit once.

"Spittin's all right," Charlie said, "if you've got the wind with you. Otherwise, it gets a little messy."

"I noticed that," said Little Harry.

Charlie seemed a little concerned. He kept looking out into the brush and toward the rocks. "Don't relax too much," he said. "Our troubles aren't over."

"I think they're just startin'," Slam Dunk said. "Two crazy guys are chasing us."

"We forgot to tell you," Dirk the Turk said. "We left a trail of blood behind us."

"I do hear dogs," Charlie said. "They sound like big ones.

"They are," said Marvin Lee, "and they've found our trail."

"Listen!" Charlie whispered.

They hushed. Suddenly the night seemed filled with noises. They came from all sides. Downstream, you could hear someone shouting threats against anyone unlucky enough to be out there in the brush.

"That's the Pouncer," Tiffany whispered. "With his dogs."

Across the river, Captain Mayhem and his troops could be heard rattling around in their armored vehicles, defending the north bank. From the south, in the distance, the sounds of an approaching automobile came closer.

"Traffic's pickin' up," Slam Dunk said.

"That's probably Captain Aguila García," Charlie said. "The Eagle of the Border. But he's not too bad. He asks questions first and shoots later—much later. And if you've got the money, he'll sell you refreshments from his cantina."

"I hear another noise," Slam Dunk said. "It's out there somewhere." He pointed to an outcropping of rocks in back of them.

"That's the one I'm worried about," Charlie said. He paused and listened. "It's either the tax collector or Bugsy and Mugsy the Tex-Mex twins." He listened again. "It's Bugsy and Mugsy," he said. "I can tell by their gruntin'. Now *they're* bad. They call themselves the Tex-Mex Connection. They shoot first and ask questions later."

"Who they lookin' for?" asked Marvin Lee.

"Me," said Charlie.

"Why?"

"I've got their suitcase," Charlie said.

That seemed a reasonable answer. If you had their suitcase, it was only natural that they should want it back. They might want to go somewhere. These kids were truly children of the border. Took things as they came. With, of course, imagination filling in the blank spots.

"Can they shoot straight?" Dirty Little Harry asked.

"They're pretty nearsighted," Charlie said.

"What happens if they don't get the suitcase?" Marvin Lee asked.

"Terrible things," Charlie said.

"Like what?"

"Like first they go crazy," Charlie said. "Then they flop on the ground and grind their teeth and roll their eyes and moan."

"Does that white stuff drip from their mouths?"

"More than likely."

"I'd like to see that," Marvin said.

"What's in the suitcase?" Tiffany asked.

"The loot, of course," said Dirty Little Harry, settling that.

"Don't say it so loud," said Charlie. "Bugsy and Mugsy will start dripping at the mouth. Then they might start shooting."

Bugsy and Mugsy weren't the only ones dripping at the mouth. Downriver, Awful Ivan's Afghans were howling like wolves. They had found the trail of blood leading right to the seat of Dirk the Turk's pants. Now Charlie was more concerned than ever. You could tell it by the way he kept watching the rocks. Sensing this, the kids moved in a little closer to him.

"We'll back you up," Marvin Lee assured Charlie.

"All the way," the others echoed.

"Thanks," said Charlie.

Talk about loyal troops. Charlie's waifs never wavered,

maybe because they knew they didn't have any choice.

If there was any wavering, it was on Charlie's part. And that was understandable. A painful—unbearable—thought had entered his mind. If he was going to save the day, or in this case the night, he had to part with a shoe. At least he had to throw something. Bugsy and Mugsy had to be put off guard, and the boulders were too big to throw. But a shoe? His runner's heart dipped at the thought and almost didn't come back up. No true runner ever parts with a shoe, not even to go to bed at night. You part with your shoes only—and only briefly—for a change of socks. Imagine, throwing away a shoe, just to save your life. Charlie had never faced a situation like this before.

The waifs were loyal but nervous. "Are we gonna run, or are we gonna die?" Dirty Little Harry asked.

"I'm thinking it over," Charlie said.

And that was when he remembered the flare pistol. It was still in his sock, where he had stuck it on his way down in the parachute. There was one cartridge left in it.

"The last flare," Charlie whispered to the group. "Get ready to run."

The bushes moved again, closer now. The voices grew louder. "Aim for his feet," Bugsy said. "Shoot him in the toe."

"Go to your marks," Charlie whispered.

The runners assumed their stance in imaginary starting blocks.

"Get set."

They rose. They waited.

Charlie shot the flare.

They split.

Running, floating, rising, falling, streaming. Charlie paced them on the sandy ground, his skinny body creating a vacuum behind him. That kept the waifs in the slipstream and made their running easier. Floating, rising, streaming. This was perhaps the nearest thing to a three-minute mile ever run, if you didn't count the ancient Incas. At the end of the mile, safe at least for the moment, Charlie pulled them up and started running in place.

"Up and down, up and down," Dirk commanded. By now, the Turk had mastered the art of winding down.

"Where's Marvin?" someone asked.

Marvin Lee was missing.

"He stopped to watch," Tiffany said.

"Watch what?" Charlie asked.

"He wanted to see them grind their teeth," Dirk said.

"And bite their tongues," added Dirty Harry.

"And maybe choke to death," said Dirk.

Just then, out of breath, Marvin Lee came streaking in and started running in place with the others. "I wanted to see 'em slobber," he said. "But . . ."

Up and down. Up and down.

"But what?" the others asked.

"But I ran head-on into another guy. Actually, I ran over him."

"What did he look like?" Charlie asked.

"Like a spook," Marvin Lee said. "Tall and floppy."

"Dressed in black?" Charlie asked.

"All over," Marvin Lee said.

"That's Grim Sam," Charlie said, "the tax collector."

"Who's he lookin' for?" Slam Dunk asked.

"Me," said Charlie.

"You sure know lots of funny people," Slam Dunk said.

"The woods are full of 'em," Charlie said.

A moment of silence. Then the big question from Dirty Little Harry. "Did you see 'em slobber?" he asked Marvin.

"Sure did," said Marvin Lee. "They almost choked to death."

Up and down. Up and down.

Nobody slept on the border that night. But then, nobody ever does. Night is heavy-traffic time, one-way traffic mostly. You never know what you'll bump into. Someday maybe they'll have stop-and-go lights. Right now, there's nothing there but stars. Plenty of those.

The traffic cops were on the job. They never give up. Awful Ivan and Halfway Hebe kept right on beating the bushes. Captain Mayhem and his troops were perched atop their tanks and trucks, sweeping the countryside with binoculars designed to penetrate the darkness. It was the latest thing in "border binocs," as the captain called them. No one knew what an object looked like at night through these binoculars, because no one had ever seen an object at night through these binoculars. These binoculars were, the troops agreed, useless. Captain Girolamo K. Mayhem loved them.

Captain Aguila García—the Eagle of the Border, who needed no binocs—was also sweeping, but not the uncharted roads. Having made his rounds, he was now tidying up the cantina which he, when not chasing smugglers, ran for their convenience. His smugglers' discount store had everything you needed, no matter which direction you were going. It was the Last Chance Cantina (if you were northbound), the First Chance (if you were southbound), and the Only Chance (if you were caught in traffic). Bugsy and Mugsy were caught in traffic. They were flopping on a table in the cantina, rolling their eyes, biting their tongues, and showing other signs of rage and discontent.

Northbound traffic was a little light that night. No grim-faced Coyotes—their pockets stuffed with money—were carrying their human cargo toward the border. Word had got around that Awful Ivan Hoffenhoff was on the prowl and that Captain Girolamo K. Mayhem was blowing smoke from both ears. When it came to the "border war," as the captain called it, he stood ready to fire at bushes and stars alike. And since there were so many of each, his guns were trained in all directions. There was nothing like a good fire storm to animate the captain. Nothing like plenty of backup troops, either. He had already alerted the Texas Rangers, the Army, the Air Force, and anybody else he could find. "An alien invasion of incredible proportions," he told them, taking Awful Ivan's word for it. The Air Force

radioed back that they had never heard of the Zacotans, or the Zobracans either, but that they would go on a Red Alert and keep the Hot Line open to the Commander in Chief, who would—if the situation required—poke the necessary buttons. No wonder no Dreamland Expresses were passing that way that night.

Huddled in their brushy retreat, Charlie and his blood-stained survivors were jubilant. Twice that night they had escaped, or so they told themselves, certain death—at least, certain capture. Now, like survivors everywhere, they were on a High, what might be called a Border High. Horseplay was in the air. Their narrow escapes became the stuff that poems are made of. They congratulated one another on their wounds, their speed, their stamina. They pretended they were bleeding to death. They described, complete with vicious snarls, what would have happened if the dogs had caught them. They feigned groans. They rolled their eyes. They even tried to slobber. Knights of the Bushes, they called themselves. Knights of the Rio Grande. Pancho Villa's Cavaliers of the Sierra Madre. Charlie's Raiders of the Mesquite Jungle.

Of course, the cactus was sticking them unmercifully, and their stamina had been less than zero since the last flight to safety, but there was no denying their speed, and even less their spirit.

The secret of their spirit was, as Charlie quickly saw, simple, and beautiful, too. As runners, they possessed a necessary, if sometimes fatal, human flaw. And that was a total disregard for reality. In the higher circles of human running, this theory was known as Charlie's Law. In the lower circles, it meant that cactus didn't stick, hunger didn't count, and exhaustion didn't exist. And so they flopped their victory flops and rolled their eyes in mockery. The Gone-Forever Mack was truly gone forever. They were what you might call the Little Left-Behinds. And though there was a world out there ready to take them apart, it wasn't here, now, in the brush. And that made all the difference. When it came to Charlie's Law, they were naturals.

Watching them arrange their world to their satisfaction, Charlie began to arrange some things to fit his own peculiar universe. Lofty goals began to swim before his eyes. A plan, rather a wild one, was beginning to form in his mind. It was a magnificent plan, as were most of Charlie's plans. But in his fanciful ramblings, where great feats were achieved against great odds, he had never dreamed anything quite like this. One reason was, no occasion like this had ever presented itself. This was simply a case of being in the right place at the right time. The Fates, though they had been a little devious at times, had been kind. They had led him intricately through a thousand terrors to this moment. It had always been, and it was still, Charlie's feet against the world. Except that now there were five other pairs of feet—and small ones at that. Six pairs of feet against the world. It was a battle cry. Trumpets sounded. Banners waved. There was glory here. Instinctively, he stretched his muscles, relaxed his breathing, slowed down his heartbeat, honed his nose, and smoothed all rough hairs in his beard, ready to run. *Bring on your glory, world.*

But Charlie did not run. Instead, he said, "Knights of the Bushes, gather round."

They gathered round. It wasn't exactly the Table Round, but the knights were no less knightly. Nor were Charlie's words any less kingly. "Knights," he said, "we have no choice. If you want to catch the Dreamland Express before it's gone forever, we've got to make a desperate run to the north. It's into the fray. And so, tomorrow night—if we don't get caught first—we're *goin' for it!*"

Not King Arthur or Pancho Villa could have chosen more knightly words.

Eyes brightened in the dark. Down the line, the words went. *Goin' for it. Goin' for it.*

The knights were properly inspired, though some were a little uncertain. "What are we goin' *for?*" Marvin asked.

Dirk the Turkish Knight of Albuquerque came to the rescue. "When you say you're goin' for it," he explained with knightly patience, "it means you're goin' for it all. You're layin' your life on the line."

"And if you don't make it," said Knight Harry of the Dirty Toes, "it means they put a bandage over your eyes and *boom!*" The Knight of the Dirty Toes was very descriptive.

"Goin' for it," Slam Dunk said, "is like the Wild Bunch when they rode into Mexico . . . in a cloud of dust."

"They got killed," said Lady Tiffany.

That did it. "Let's go for it!" the Knights of the Bushes squeaked. "North to Blanco Canyon!" They were on the verge of hysteria. *Bring on your glory, world.*

"I was thinking more like Albuquerque," Charlie said. The greater the distance, the greater the glory.

"*Albuquerque!*" The ungrateful knights were in rebellion. "That's five hundred miles."

Albuquerque. Santa Fe. The Canadian border. It was all the same to Charlie. With kingly generosity, he waved his hands in the air and said, "Wherever."

"Right on," the others cried. "To Blanco Canyon."

The revolt of the knights was over.

Goin' for it. The words never failed to light Charlie's fire. But the Old Knight of the Dunes and Thistles, who wasn't much over thirty, had a few things to take care of before they went for it. Otherwise, his First Law—the total disregard for reality—might break down in midflight. He was thinking of the necessities, all those little things that give you the edge. Food, water, running gear, shoes—especially shoes. The Little Knights of the Mesquite Meadows, for all their gallantry in action, were practically shoeless. How they had managed to run this far was a mystery. And though their tattered clothes might stream well in the wind, they weren't made for boiling suns and cool desert nights. It was not his wish to litter the desert with casualties. No glory there.

King Charlie set to work on his shopping list. "Man the battlements," he said to the knights.

"Battlements?" asked Dirk the puzzled Turkish Knight.

"He means the watchtowers," said Lady Tiffany.

"Which means the weeds," said Slam the Knight of the Dunks.

They poked their heads up through the weeds, while King Charlie went on dreaming up his shopping list.

Little canteens, the King was thinking, with—but no, there was no Gatorade in Mexico.

"I think there's something moving out there," Lady Tiffany said.

King Charlie grunted, still thinking: Water is better anyway . . . unless it's Mexican water, which it looks like it will be . . . at least for a while . . . Maybe we can find a horse tank later . . . and in the meantime a little Pepto-Bismol.

The shadows kept moving in the brush.

"I think there's something we ought to tell you," the Knight of the Dunks whispered to the King.

King Charlie grunted again, still thinking: Forty hard miles of rough terrain . . . hills and valleys . . . mesquite and chaparral . . . jagged rocks . . . a long and steady run . . . the right shoes . . . the right survival gear . . .

"Are those humans or animals or just shadows moving around out there?" Knight Marvin Lee asked Lady Tiffany.

"They're human shadows," said Knight Harry of the Dirty Toes. "We had better warn the King."

"The King is lost in thought," said Lady Tiffany.

. . . There would be the sun . . . There would be the hot sand . . . and the cactus . . . and the wind . . . and maybe the rain . . . But no, no rain . . . Not this time of year . . . Midsummer . . . So the clothes would have to fit loose . . . No drag . . . Something in the Arabian fashion . . . with the breeze coming in and the heat going out.

Finally, the King got it all together in his mind. "The Sweet Life Discount Store," he cried. "Captain Aguila García's emporium for hard-pressed humans. First, we get the survival gear. Then we try to keep out of jail until we're ready to go for it. That's the basic plan."

The King seemed pleased.

But the knights were nervous. Those shadows were still moving.

"Charlie," Slam Dunk said, forgetting his royal manners, "I think we're pretty close to going to jail right now."

Actually, they were closer than they knew. For in that

instant a pack of Afghans came lunging into the hideout, their long tails in the air and their hot tongues out.

"It's my blood they want!" Dirk cried.

And it seemed they did. They had the little guy down and were pummeling him unmercifully. Dogs' tongues and dogs' tails were everywhere. So were their claws. Everybody was stumbling over everybody else. Marvin had hold of one of the long tails and was trying with no luck to pull a beast off Dirk. Dirk was gripping the dog's jaws, trying to hold them shut. But the big tongue and hot breath kept coming back out. Something about the blood tended to excite their savage natures.

"Step on their toes!" Charlie shouted. "They'll back off."

The trouble was, the kids' feet were more tender than the dogs' toes. Mostly, it was the dogs stepping on the kids' toes. Those claws were really tearing things up.

But the worst was yet to come. From out of somewhere— a bush, a tree, a cloud, who knows from where—Awful Ivan Hoffenhoff came pouncing from above.

"Watch out for knives!" he cried to Halfway Hebe. "The savages will cut out your heart!"

Awful Ivan had pounced mostly on the dogs. And then Halfway Hebe, a bit behind in everything, had pounced on Awful Ivan. In the darkness, you couldn't tell dogs from humans, not even by their howls. Awful Ivan had his handcuffs out, waving them wildly, crying, "Surrender! Surrender!" After a struggle, he managed to get one of the handcuffs on Halfway Hebe and the other on the hind leg of a dog. But by that time both Ivan and his sub-constable were hung up in a vicious yucca plant.

That was when King Charlie, making sure he had all the noble knights, bolted for safety—followed by a couple of the more playful hounds, still snapping at the seat of Dirk's pants.

In disarray, the Knights of the Bushes Round were fleeing through Thistle Forest, temporarily routed.

5

If it's disaster you're looking for, try Bugsy and Mugsy the Tex-Mex twins. They're natural disasters, asleep or awake. Right at the moment, they were asleep, feet on the table, shoeless and sockless. Captain Aguila García, always on the alert, had slipped their shoes from their feet, just in case they forgot to pay their bill. As for socks, they never wore them—saved on the laundry bill. It was best, if you could keep from it, not to mess with Bugsy and Mugsy. Unfortunately for Charlie and his waifs, they were running headlong into just such a mess. And even more unfortunately, Charlie was carrying that suitcase full of money.

"What are you gonna spend the money on?" little Tiffany asked Charlie.

"Running shoes," he said.

That made sense to Tiffany.

Now, as they neared the Sweet Life Discount Store, Charlie swung his party of dogs and kids around the outer rims. He was not one to go barging into disaster. He always circled, keeping up speed, while looking for friendly signs and welcome mats—particularly at the back door. Charlie knew how suitcases full of anything have a way of opening back doors on the border. The trick was to get the right person—usually called Our Man in Mexico—to open the door, and then to keep on circling the little planet of thieves and smugglers until you could see, plainly in the starlight, the welcome mat come flying out. If that didn't happen, you kept on circling, except that the circles got wider and wider, until finally you were safely circling somewhere in outer space.

Another turn, and still another turn.

"We're circling the moon," Marvin Lee puffed.

"Keep the after-burners burning," Charlie said.

"My after-burner's shot," said Dirk the Turk.

Two turns later, it came. Captain Aguila García—everybody's Man in Mexico—stood at the back door, the welcome mat held high. "*Bienvenidos!*" Waving cheerfully, he said, "Señor Suitcase Charlie Jones. Come in. Let me relieve you of your luggage."

Charlie circled in, kids and dogs behind him.

"Run in place. Run in place," Dirk commanded. "Up and down. Up and down."

As they wound down, Captain García wound up, cheery

and chattery. He got lonely on nights when the traffic was slow. "Señor Charlie, it is good to see you. I heard you fell from an airplane fatally. And I heard other disasters as well. I did not know you had so many children, or dogs either. Who are these little cavaliers with the dirty noses? They look like they just got off a boat from China."

"We fell off a truck," Marvin Lee said.

"And bounced," Dirk added.

"Many do," the Eagle said. "It's a good thing that children bounce. Ah, the sad tales I could tell you about all the bouncing children. Kids lost on both sides of the river. Sometimes I think there is a lost kid under every mesquite bush." Lowering his voice, the captain said to Charlie, "You have enemies in the front room. But have no fear. I will slip you into the back room."

"We're also being pursued," Charlie said.

"Ah, yes, the Pouncer," Captain García said. "I have heard he is out tonight. On a rampage. Looking for Zacotans, they say." The captain tapped his head. "And they tell me the tax collector is also circulating." Captain García was holding two pairs of alligator shoes. "Would you like to buy these?" he asked. "Tuccis. Imported from Tijuana. They came from the feet of two notorious stiffs."

"Dead men?" Charlie asked.

"No, alas," the Eagle sighed. "Just stiff men. They will thaw out before sunrise."

Switching quickly over to business, Captain García conducted Charlie and the waifs into the back room, where the search for survival gear began.

This was not the happiest place in the world to look for such things. It appeared that most of the people who had once worn these items had not survived. To Charlie, it seemed a storehouse of bartered dreams and vanished hopes—in all sizes. There was no describing the aroma of the garments, though it, too, hinted strongly of human desperation. Still, if you didn't get lost in the stacks of contraband and choke to death, you could find anything you wanted. "Only the best," the captain said, "from Taiwan, Hong Kong, Singapore, and the Land of the Rising Sun. Some are slightly used, as you can see by the bullet holes."

Charlie set to work picking among the treasures. When it came to survival gear, he was the master picker. He had picked through every discount survival store on the continent. And the waifs, he found out, were little masters, too. In the fine art of dressing for survival, they knew what clothes they would and would not be found dead in. So Charlie let them pick—battle gear, jungle gear, desert gear, whatever Sweet Life fashions they could find. Except, of course, the shoes. "No high heels," he told little Tiffany. "Or cowboy boots," he cautioned Marvin. "Take off the wedgies, Dirk."

Charlie picked on. The kids picked on. Despite the smell, it was a room of endless treasures. Anything your heart desired. And a lot of things your heart did not desire. When Charlie had picked the small canteens, complete with the finest Mexican water, and the Pepto-Bismol, and the small tins of Spam, and the sardines, and the crackers and the cheese and the bread, and the tiny flashlights with Japanese batteries MADE, it said on the label, IN TIJUANA, he turned his attention to the most serious thing of all, saying, "Now, about those shoes . . . the *force majeure*, to put it in the ancient Incan tongue."

"Put precisely," Captain García agreed.

Precisely put or not, this was too important an item to leave to the whims of fashion. Charlie was one of the few people on earth who understood the twenty-six bones in the human foot. He even knew how they connected to the human mind, both conscious and subconscious. It was his *edge.* And so he went to work on the dirty feet, humming *Give It All You've Got* when pleased, frowning slightly when displeased. He popped toes, snapped arches, wiggled ankles, and coaxed a few reluctant bones back in their proper sockets.

"I would observe," the captain said to Charlie, "that you still have a thing with feet."

"Your observation is correct," said Charlie.

"I would say they turn you on."

"Put precisely," said Charlie, popping another toe.

Give It All You've Got, he hummed, trumpets sounding in his ears. *Go for it!* There was no margin for error here. Piles of shoes lay around him in colorful disarray. The Whole Earth Shoe Factory had deposited its treasures on the floor. If a runner couldn't find the right survival shoe in that glorious pile, he didn't deserve to survive.

"Where is the Inca Zephyr, made of the finest llama?" Charlie asked the captain.

"Right here, señor," Captain García replied, handing him an Australian Floater made of the wallaby kangaroo.

Charlie tossed it on the reject pile.

"How about this Filipino Water Buffalo Streaker?" the captain asked, handing Charlie what was obviously a Wildebeest Courser from Africa.

On the reject pile.

"Or this Aztec Adder from the pits of Montezuma?"

On the reject pile.

Finally, to his delight, and to the relief of Captain García, Charlie found what he was looking for—the Hopi Indian Smoker, made of something known only to the Hopis. It had both speed and distance. But more than that, it had survival. With it, the Hopis had outrun all conquistadors, ancient and modern.

"Feet!" Charlie commanded. The squad advanced, feet forward. "No dogs," he said, pushing the Afghans aside.

A few minutes later, the little runners were wearing Hopi Smokers—and just about everything else the human mind could imagine. While Charlie had been concentrating on the shoes, they had piled on several layers of survival gear, taking no chances. Ski pants, gas masks, bush jackets, berets, combat ponchos, you name it. When Charlie stood them up for inspection, they resembled nothing so much as some tattered international brigade of refugees who had crossed a desert to come to grief right there in the back room of a Mexican cantina. All that was missing was a dead camel or two.

"Good Lord!" cried Charlie.

"Mother of God!" cried Captain García.

"You like it, huh?" they asked.

How could you keep from liking it? It was beyond liking. It was beautiful. It was breathtaking. They had left off only one indispensable item. "Where are the Arabian head shawls?" Charlie asked.

"Behind the camel hides, of course," said Captain García.

"Bring them out," Charlie ordered.

"The camel hides?"

"The head shawls."

Captain García brought them out. "These are from an

ill-fated caravan," he said. "So are the camel hides. I hope the thought does not depress you?"

Nothing could depress the little sheikhs as they snapped up the Arabian head shawls. Hopi Smokers and Arabian head shawls. Who could ask for more? Dirty Little Harry could. "Where are the daggers?" he asked.

"And the white nightgowns?" Dirk asked.

"And the beads?" asked Tiffany.

But gowns and beads were out. For in that moment, as Charlie was paying the bill, Captain García leaned over and whispered to him, "It is not my wish to spoil our transaction, Señor Charlie, but I see four huge bare feet standing behind us at the door. They belong, I believe, to human animals."

"How many toes do they have?" Charlie asked.

"More than the Good Lord intended, I think. To avoid trouble, and maybe bloodshed too, perhaps I had better arrest them, on some pretext or another."

"Good thinking," Charlie said.

"There is only one small problem, a technicality really."

"What is that?"

"They are pointing guns at us."

"What are their intentions?"

"I will inquire," the captain said. "But first let me tell you that my floor is full of vicious splinters. To walk on it barefooted can be painful, perhaps fatal. You will note how they stand there hopping. Also I must tell you that my little cantina has many doors. Front doors. Back doors. Side doors. It was built that way to facilitate departures in situations like this. I would suggest that you and the dogs and the children try to slip out a window, while I cleverly divert the enemy."

That would take some slipping. The kids were so loaded down with survival gear that they couldn't have squeezed through a door, much less a window. The dogs might have made it. But the dogs seemed unconcerned. They just stood there wagging their tails, perhaps protectively. The kids themselves, fascinated, were staring at Bugsy and Mugsy.

"I saw you guys slobber," Marvin Lee said, through a gas mask he was wearing.

"Are you gonna shoot us?" Dirty Little Harry asked.

"We don't shoot kids," Bugsy said.

"Naw," said Mugsy. "Just the big guys. Like that skinny one back there with the wings on his feet."

"He's wearin' bulletproof clothes," said Dirk.

"He better be wearin' armor plate," said Bugsy.

"And he better have a suitcase," Mugsy said.

"And it better be full."

"You guys look mean," Dirty Little Harry said.

"We are," the Tex-Mex twins said together. "Meaner than us you won't find."

"Your toes are funny," Marvin Lee said.

"Don't make jokes, kid," Bugsy said.

Up till now, the kids had been "diverting" the enemy. Now, while Charlie kept his back turned, looking in vain for concealed doors, Captain Aguila García came cheerfully into the game. "Amigos of the Queer Toes," he said, "what are your intentions?"

"We aim to maim," said Bugsy.

"Unless we get the loot, we shoot," said Mugsy.

"And we want our Tuccis, too," said Bugsy.

Captain García was still holding the alligator shoes. "Ah, these glossy items of vulgarity," he said. "But first you must pay your bill. Two tequilas—that is, five hundred dollars."

"Chicken feed," said Mugsy. "We're big spenders."

"We never quibble," said Bugsy.

"Our money's in the suitcase," Mugsy said. "Hand over the suitcase, and we hand over the money."

"First the money," said the captain.

"First the suitcase," said the twins.

"No money, no suitcase," said the captain.

"No suitcase, no money," said the twins.

"What we have here," the Eagle of the Border said, "is a standoff. Please bear with me while I confer with my colleague. By the way, there is someone standing behind you, and he is holding a gun."

"That's an old trick," Bugsy said. "How dumb do you think we are?"

How dumb they were, nobody really knew. But it was a fact that Grim Sam the tax collector was standing behind them. And he was holding a gun. Now it was a kind of three-way standoff.

There are worse things. One of them is a three-way shoot-out. Another is a three-way shoot-out where all the guns are on one side.

"Amigo," Captain García whispered to Charlie, "we are in serious trouble. I fear you are almost dead."

"Are you sure there's a door here somewhere?" Charlie asked, stumbling through crates of contraband.

"It is a concealed door, Señor Charlie—very concealed. Look behind the fake Persian rugs. If it is not there, it will be behind the fake Italian bedspreads. It is there some-where. Try peeling off a little wallpaper."

"I think I've found it," Charlie said. "Is it made of fake plywood?"

"Naturally."

Charlie coaxed the door open, spilling contraband, fake and otherwise, half in and half out of the opening. Then quickly he jumped back, closing the door as best he could behind him. "It's that crazy Pouncer!" he said to the captain. "Stand by for a crash."

"We're surrounded," said the Eagle cheerfully. "But never fear. I have trapdoors in the floor, if I can locate them."

Charlie didn't much like the thought of being trapped in a basement.

"Look under the fake Brazilian coffee beans," the captain said. "'There was a trapdoor there the last time I looked— about twenty years ago," he added.

But the fake Brazilian coffee beans went undisturbed. There wasn't time to dislodge them. Awful Ivan Hoffen-hoff—followed by Halfway Hebe, a pair of handcuffs swinging from his wrist—crashed through the fake plywood door and landed in a heap on the fake Italian bedspreads. "Za-cotans!" he shouted, firing a shotgun blast through the ceiling, just before disappearing beneath a sea of sheets and pillowcases.

"As the saying goes," said Captain García, "it seems we have killed three birds with one stone."

And it seems that he was right. In a sense, Awful Ivan had saved the day. For he had taught the Afghans to pounce at the sound of gunfire. It didn't matter which direction they pounced or on what they pounced, so long as they pounced. Just like Ivan himself. And that was what happened here. Hearing the shotgun blast, the dogs bounded through the air and came to rest on the twins and the tax collector. Their great tails were in the air. Snarls could be heard from their hot mouths. They seemed to relish the thought of chewing up fat little gangsters and spooky tax collectors.

"Call 'em off!" the twins cried, in unison.

"Call 'em off!" cried the tax collector.

"Sic 'em!" hissed Dirty Little Harry.

"Go get 'em," said Dirk the Turk.

"White stuff's drippin' from their lips," said Marvin Lee.

"The dogs, or the victims?" asked Dirty Little Harry.

"Both," said Marvin Lee.

"Call 'em off!" the twins shouted again.

But no one knew exactly how to call the dogs off, so no one bothered. And besides, it was time to go. Charlie started gathering up his survivors of the Battle of the Cantina. Captain García, a tear in his eagle eye, though still cheerful, stepped forward. "Señor Charlie," he said, "I must apologize for this disruption. If you come this way again, I shall see that things are more civilized. Also, as my duty commands, I shall have to chase you around the bushes a bit, to make my superiors think I am earning my pay and my pension. I'm sure you understand."

"I understand," said Charlie.

"We understand, too," the kids said. "We're supposed to be on one side and you're supposed to be on the other."

"Put precisely," said the Eagle of the Border. "Things do tend to get mixed up. Now let me embrace you and send you on your way with my blessings and good wishes, both of which you will need. By morning, the pursuers will be after you again. And once you start to the north, others will hound you, too. I have been told that troops are being deployed to intercept you. A general alert is out. There will be the border patrol and the river patrol and the desert patrol and maybe the highway patrol. If you beat them all, with nothing but your own two feet, your names will be sung in glory on this sad border, and your deed recounted."

"That's nice to know," said Charlie. "And if we don't make it?"

"Then your deeds will be sung even more gloriously. That is the way the world works."

Charlie looked around him. "There is just one other thing. Where did I put that suitcase?"

"Ah! the suitcase. To be sure," the captain said. He threw back a pile of fake Australian sheepskins. "For safe-keeping," he said, "in case you had to depart in haste. Would you like to leave it with me? I will hide it behind one of my concealed doors."

"Thank you," Charlie said. "I believe I will."

Charlie gathered his troops around him and went out through the back door. There he was joined by two happy Afghans, each with a gun in its mouth. As the runners started to trot, the dogs dropped the guns and lifted their noses, the children dropped a little of their survival gear and let the breeze brush their faces. Slowly the little group began to circle, each lap around the cantina growing wider. In a little while the pace picked up and they were moving safely again in outer space.

Circling the moon.

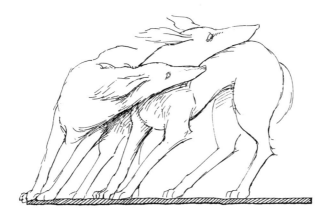

Sunrise on the border. Hiding time. Restoration time. Break out the food. Any kind of food.

"Pass the Spam," Marvin Lee said, tearing open a great loaf of the hardest bread ever baked, "and a hammer if you've got one."

"For that bread," Slam Dunk said, "you'll need a hacksaw."

All the mouths were full, including those of the dogs. The feast was on. You can only run so far without food, and they had just about reached their limit. Sleep, which they badly needed too, would come later. They were hiding at the bottom of a deep ditch, covered with weeds, a short distance from the river. Sunrise, hunger, and weariness had caught up with them at about the same time.

"Pass the sardines," Dirk the Turk requested, "and the cheese and the crackers and the butter and the salami and anything else you've got." Dirk was wrestling with a loaf of bread in the sand. On top of him was a dog. Sand was flying in all directions.

Everybody was smacking. Grit, sand, dirt, weeds, it didn't matter what the bread had in it, or on it, so long as they could cover it up with butter—or what passed for butter.

"Best butter I ever ate," Marvin said, stuffing his mouth. "Must be goat."

"I don't think it's butter," Tiffany said. "Looks more like lard."

"It's go-o-ood," Dirty Little Harry said.

"So's this cheese," Marvin said. "Green, but go-o-ood."

For some reason, the Afghans turned up their noses at the cheese, and didn't seem all that excited about the butter, either. It was the Spam they were after. They seemed to have a knack for intercepting it between the tin and the bread it was supposed to go on.

"Go easy on the water," Charlie cautioned. "Take it in small dribbles."

"I already had a big swig," Marvin Lee said, burping noisily. He rolled his eyes in mock agony. "You think I'll die?"

"Prob'ly," Dirty Little Harry said, yanking his Spam back from the teeth of a dog.

No doubts about their spirits. A total disregard for reality, which meant an innocent disregard for life and limb—and the stomach in particular.

"Now," said Charlie, when the smacking had quieted a little and the dogs were yawning, "tonight we head north."

"Into the wilds of Texas," Slam Dunk said.

"With a little luck," Charlie went on, "we'll be safe here the rest of the day. Normally, this would be cactus-picking time, but things aren't normal."

Charlie was thinking of Awful Ivan and the Tex-Mex twins. Madmen, he knew, never sleep, even under the most comfortable piles of fake Italian bedspreads. Nor do gangsters linger long on splintered floors where dogs have left them mangled. Madmen rise up, the bedspreads with them, and rage into the dawn. Gangsters do the same, even if it means wearing wedgies instead of Tuccis. As for tax collectors, no one knows what they will do.

"Here's the plan," Charlie said. "It comes from chapter I of the *Survivor's Manual* and is known as the Runner's Ritual. You always carry it out before you start the big run. First—and this is very important—get plenty of sleep. Don't just sleep any old way. Relax every muscle in your body. Sleep like a cat. You can even purr if you want to. When you wake up, just before sundown, do the stretches and swings and warm-ups, rinse out your mouths with water, inspect your shoes, and check your food supply. Reduce your survival gear to the barest minimum. Bury what you don't need. Then strap on your packs and canteens. The main thing is, dress for speed and endurance—"

"We got plenty of that," Dirk interrupted.

"Yeah," echoed Little Harry. "We got speed to burn."

"You'll need it," Charlie said. "And maybe a little more, too." He went on with the instructions. "Just after dark, we slip across the river. Then we observe, waiting for the right moment. When the right moment comes, we head out across a long stretch of flatland, mostly desert, in Indian file. There is a range of hills on the left. If we have to take cover there, we will. We go low and slow at first, just warmin' up, gettin' our second wind. When we get that, the speed picks up, and we start floatin' through the night across Texas."

"Like ghosts," said Slam Dunk.

"Exactly," said Charlie. "It's what you might call a ghostly forty-mile run. Floating by night and hiding by day."

"Couldn't we go nonstop?" Marvin asked.

Charlie ignored that. The forty miles covered some of the worst terrain on earth. The temperature during the day was always around 110°. And if the weather started doing unpredictable things, there was no describing the dangers that lay ahead. Charlie left that part out—the sandstorms, the quick drops in temperature at night—knowing that horror stories are not always the most inspiring stories, though with these kids he might easily have been wrong.

"Now," he concluded, "that's the way we do it."

And that was the way they did it. They slept like cats until evening, the Afghans watching over them. Nightfall found them making their way to the river. They were slimmed down now—streamlined, not one ounce of excess baggage on them. In the shadows, you might have taken them for ancient Incans. Or maybe Comanches. Of course, if you looked at their heads, they looked like nomads from Arabia, skirting some waterhole at dusk and very mindful of some enemy that might lurk there. Cautiously, they slipped along, followed by the Afghans. No one spoke. Their eyes were on the river and, as much as they could see in the growing darkness, beyond.

Silently, they eased along the stream, until they found a narrow spot with little water. Then they slid across and up the opposite bank, poking their heads over the edge. The main force of Captain Girolamo K. Mayhem's troops was nowhere in sight. But there were plenty of patrol cars prowling up and down. Their radios crackled, disturbing the night.

"So far, so good," Charlie whispered. "Now we observe."

What they observed was, to say the least, unsettling. One of the patrol cars made a slow turn and drove along the river's edge, flashing spotlights over the bushes on both sides. As it approached them, it slowed even more, then came to a stop. They could have reached out and touched it—if, that is, by some means known only to children, they hadn't managed to sink at least a foot deeper into the sand and, for good measure, make themselves invisible. At least, they hoped they were invisible.

Charlie wasn't invisible, but he was cool—real cool. He recognized the two agents in the car. Everybody on the border knew them. They belonged to the corps of Bushmen. Very aptly named. Heavy-browed creatures. Not much given to humor, on or off the job. Not much given to anything except kicking and whacking bushes. Which was how they got their names of Bushkicker and Bushwhacker. Between the two of them, they had kicked and whacked every bush between Socorro and Laredo. If there had been no bushes in the world to kick, with people under them, Bushkicker and Bushwhacker would have died of boredom, or perhaps a broken heart. They were to kicking and whacking what Awful Ivan was to pouncing. With them around, nobody was safe under any bush anywhere.

"Well, now," Bushkicker said, "I guess we better get out and kick the bushes around a little—see if a few heads roll."

"Suppose so," said Bushwhacker.

They couldn't have missed. If Bushkicker had just stepped out of the patrol car, he would have set his big boot on Marvin's head. Marvin's head probably couldn't have stood that. His head was already a foot beneath the surface, and going down. With Bushkicker on it, it would have sunk to the water level.

Bushkicker had the car door open, one leg out, when the radio opened up.

"Come in, Bushmen! Come in, Bushmen! This is Chief Bushman Mayhem calling. Over!"

"It's the big bush," Bushwhacker said. "Better answer him, or he'll go crazy."

"I'd rather kick bushes," Bushkicker said. "And besides, he's already crazy."

Talk to him, Charlie thought. *Talk to him. Just don't set that foot down.*

"Bushmen! Bushmen! Come in, Bushmen of the Lower Order!" the radio blared forth. "This is your superior calling. I have urgent messages. Over!"

"If you don't answer him," Bushwhacker said, "he'll think we're down at the Chinese Fast Food Pizza and Taco Pagoda."

Answer him, Charlie pleaded silently. *Answer him.*

"He called us Lower-Order Bushmen," Bushkicker said. "I don't much appreciate that." But he answered. "Go ahead, Chief Bushman, sir. What is your position? Over."

"I'll ask the questions!" Chief Bushman Mayhem roared back. "Stand by for messages. Over."

"I hate that guy," Bushkicker said. "We kick all the bushes and he gets all the glory. He's prob'ly sittin' up there somewhere on his cherry picker lookin' through his night binocs and talkin' to the Commander in Chief of National Bush Control—with his battle plans flyin' in the breeze."

Captain Girolamo K. Mayhem was indeed high up in his cherry picker. And his battle plans were indeed flying in the breeze. He was looking through his night binocs, seeing nothing. The captain had a whole regiment of cherry pickers—of the hydraulic kind—which he could swing out over the river and look down from, always seeing nothing. With luck, and plenty of hydraulic fluid, he could get ten feet over Mexico—and still see nothing. All because of those night binocs. Of all his peculiar gadgetry, Captain Mayhem most doted on his cherry pickers and his night binocs. With them in action, he could report back to headquarters, unfailingly, that the border was "clean."

"Go ahead," Bushkicker said over the radio.

"I'll go ahead when I'm ready to go ahead," Mayhem cried from his cherry picker. "Don't be telling me when to go ahead. Now—I'm ready to go ahead. Urgent messages. Check all checkpoints. Keep all channels open. Look out for footprints. Be on lookout for infiltrating Zacotans."

"Who the—!"

"Don't say it, don't say it," Bushwhacker said. "You know how mean he gets about foul language on the airwaves. He'll have us up for polluting, or something worse."

Bushkicker gnashed his teeth. "Who are the Zacotans? Over."

"Alien intruders, you simpleton!" Mayhem cried. "They are being pursued by Constable Hoffenhoff, one of our more

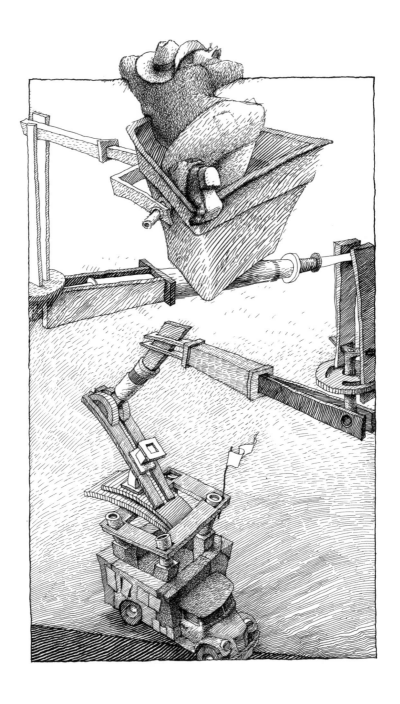

dedicated spies. Word has it that they are hiding in your area—probably right under your noses."

Marvin's head went deeper into the sand. His ears were about covered up. All the others were holding their breath.

"Hoffenhoff," Bushkicker said to Bushwhacker. "He's crazier than Mayhem."

"Impossible," Bushwhacker said.

"Ain't he the one that's always seein' flying saucers?" Bushkicker asked.

"That's the one," Bushwhacker said. "We chased those things all over Texas."

"Now we're after Zacotans. Wonder what they look like." Bushkicker went back on the air. "More information requested," he said. "More details about Zacotans. Over."

Mayhem's radio popped and crackled. "Part of the Zobra Clan," he explained. "Related to the Zobracans and Zapatans. Be on alert. They shoot with poison darts . . . Don't turn your back . . . Arrest everybody in sight . . . O-oo-oops!"

"What's that?" Bushkicker cried over the air.

"Wind got under my maps," Mayhem said. "I'm up high, you know."

It sounded as if he was high. Sounded as if he was out of sight. "Over and out," Bushkicker said, trying to escape the captain's onslaught of names, maps, cherry pickers, and Border Highs.

"Don't *out* me!" Mayhem shouted. "I'll do the outing. Out!" he said.

It seemed that everybody was high that night. Half the continent was high and going higher. Except for the fugitives with their heads a foot beneath the sand and going lower.

But suddenly they got a break. Bushkicker lifted his big leg, pulled it back inside, and slammed the door.

Now, thought Charlie, *they will go. Now*, thought the heads beneath the sand, *they will go.*

They started, but then they stopped. Another patrol car, lights flashing and sirens screaming, pulled up alongside the first one. "We got a bulletin," the driver of the second car said. "From the Commandant of Bush Control."

"What would he know about kicking bushes?" Bushkicker asked.

"The bulletin says we can't pursue the Zacotans beyond the Rio Grande."

"Why not?" Bushwhacker asked.

"Yak fever," the driver said. "It's catching."

"You ever had it?" Bushkicker asked.

"I been inoculated," the driver said.

"It's carried on bushes," his partner said.

"Very fatal," the driver said, racing his motor and spinning his wheels before pulling out in a cloud of dust.

Not to be outdone, Bushkicker raced his motor and spun his wheels and pulled out in a cloud of dust behind them.

Up out of the sand came dogs, Charlie, children, half suffocated.

"Watch out for Zacotans," Tiffany said.

"Don't touch the bushes," said Marvin.

"We might get yak fever," said Dirk.

"I been inoculated," Dirty Little Harry said.

Their spirits were still up. They had survived the first encounter.

"Now," said Charlie, "fall in behind me. Slam Dunk will bring up the rear. We start out slow and easy, the wind in our faces." Charlie could hear the trumpets in his ears.

And the kids must have heard something, too. "We're goin' for it," they whispered, as the patrol cars disappeared in the distance.

And they went for it, floating through the night.

Like ghosts.

Into the desert night. Under a million stars. Under a smugglers' moon. North to Blanco Canyon. No manmade terrors here. Only the clean-sweet smell of sage. This was a runners' world.

Charlie led his Magnificent Seven—counting the Afghans—on one of the best five-mile glides ever run. A kind of warm-up for the big show. He had paced them perfectly on the flat terrain. They were running silently and smoothly, their Arabian head shawls streaming in the breeze. Bells were ringing in Charlie's ears, to mix with the sound of flügelhorns. *Bring on your pursuers, world.*

They ran until Charlie could hear the first faint signs of weariness. Then slowly he dropped the pace, bringing them finally to a halt.

"Up and down. Up and down."

Dutifully they obeyed the Turk, everyone except the dogs, who flopped down flat. But almost before hitting the ground, one of the dogs came back up, his great tail out, his nose in the air, whimpering.

"What's the matter with him?" Tiffany asked.

The other dog shot up, bristling.

"Wait here," Charlie said. "And keep your muscles loose." Then he stepped off the trail and laid his ear to the ground. He could hear his little samurai as they stretched their legs in the ritual of relaxation. And then he heard something else. No wonder the dogs had sniffed some alien presence on the air. It was the steady, rhythmic pat of a single pair of feet. The runner, a poor one, had a limp. The bells stopped ringing in Charlie's ears. Back at the runners' circle, he said, "It's the Apache Stalker. He's found our trail."

"*Oh!*"

That was the best they could do. But since the "*Oh*" had a choking sound, and the sound of fear as well, that was plenty. None of them had ever heard of the Apache Stalker, but any Apache anywhere who was stalking anybody anywhere was something to keep away from.

"Maybe we go nonstop after all," Marvin Lee said, breathing hard.

"Maybe we take him in a trap," Dirty Little Harry said, spitting air.

"An Apache? In a trap?" Slam Dunk marveled. Everyone marveled.

"And plant him in an anthill," Dirty Harry persisted. The kid was merciless.

So was Dirk the Turk. It was a contest of ideas. "We could use scorpions," he said.

"How?" Little Harry asked, genuinely interested.

"I haven't figured that part out yet," said Dirk.

Charlie intervened. "Those are all very pleasant suggestions," he said, "but it's really too late now."

"You mean he's closin' in for the kill?" Dirk asked.

"For the slaughter," Harry corrected.

"I mean," Charlie said, "that he's already radioed back to the border patrol. Any moment now, the alert will go out. Right now, he's just keepin' track of us. He's what you call an informer."

"You mean a snitch?" Marvin Lee asked.

"That's what I mean," Charlie said.

"He oughta be shot," Dirty Little Harry said.

"He has been, several times," Charlie said. "That's why he limps."

"Why is he called the Apache Stalker?" Tiffany asked.

"That's what he calls himself," Charlie said. "He's real nutty. Fancies himself an Apache. Wears leggins, moccasins, everything Apache style. He's probably never seen an Apache. His real name's Ellsworth."

There was a noticeable sigh of relief. If you had your choice of stalkers, you'd take Ellsworth any time. Only Dirty Harry seemed disappointed. "Maybe we could just punch him out," he said.

Just about the same time Harry said "punch," someone

somewhere far in back of them punched a button. The alert was out. Sirens wailed. Lights began to flash. Cars and jeeps roared along the river road. Ellsworth the Snitch—alias the Apache Stalker—had done his dirty work.

Bring on your pursuers, world.

And the world brought them on. That rang Charlie's bell anew. He liked the odds, which were not entirely in his favor. Made him feel like a kid again, when the odds against you were stacked sky-high. And besides, he had not run blindly into this situation. Charlie never ran blindly into any situation. That was his Second Law. Now he knew exactly what he and the Magnificent Seven had to do. "We've got to get the Stalker's radio," he said. "And we've got to do it fast."

In the distance, the cars and jeeps were pulling out, sirens wailing.

"Here's what we do," Charlie said. The Seven Samurai waited, eager to play deadly games. "We circle the Apache Stalker—"

"Call him by that other name," Tiffany said.

"Okay," said Charlie. "We circle Ellsworth. Then we move in from all sides. First one there tackles him by both legs. The others come screaming in on top of him."

"Who takes the scalp?" Dirty Little Harry asked.

"Just take the radio," Charlie said. "And watch out for that musket he carries. It goes off when you least expect it. When we get the radio, turn him loose and watch him go smokin' for the border."

"That's when we put the dogs on him," Dirk said.

"Good thinkin'," Charlie said. "But don't worry. The dogs'll be there anyway. Afghans love to romp."

"Are you sure he's not an Apache?" Slam Dunk asked.

"Or something worse? I was thinking of knives, and certain ceremonies."

"Positive," Charlie said. "In fact, his last name is Flake—Ellsworth Flake."

"We can't miss," Dirk said.

The truth was, his last name was Higgins. He had once been a bank clerk, and later, one thing leading to another, a convict. But Charlie always grew poetic with names in moments of great danger. Flake sounded about as threatening as ice cream. Had to keep the spirits high. The higher the spirit, the lower the casualty rate.

"Let's move out," Charlie said. "Slam Dunk, Dirk, and Harry to the left. I'll take Tiff and Marvin to the right. Dogs down the middle. When we get close, I'll scream 'Cut the Stalker's throat!' That will unnerve him. Then we attack. If his gun goes off, the dogs will get him. If it doesn't go off, we will get him. Either way, we've got him."

Dirty Little Harry made a gagging sound to show what would happen once they had him.

They moved out, their minds a mixture of fearful words like Apache Stalker and less fearful ones like Ellsworth Flake. From one extreme to the other. About a hundred yards down the trail, they saw him, or at least they saw a shadow. In the dark, the shadow looked like a true Apache. He was down on one knee examining the trail. His musket was pointed skyward. The moment was perfect.

"Cut the Stalker's throat!" Charlie screamed.

The gun went off. The dogs came flying in. The kids came flying in. It was short and it was furious, a mass of arms, legs, claws, and teeth. The bodies got entangled. The bodies got disentangled. Then they got entangled again. When they got disentangled the second time, the Apache

Stalker was fleeing southward toward the border, the dogs in hot pursuit, and Charlie was pushing every button he could find on the portable radio. Which was where things started falling apart.

The radio batteries were weak, almost gone, and there was so much shouting on the other end of the line that Captain Mayhem couldn't hear Charlie. Most of the shouting was coming from the captain himself. As usual, he wanted to give all the orders, reprimand all the troops, carry out all the battle plans, and, if any were taken, execute all the prisoners. Somewhere high up in his cherry picker, his maps flying in the wind, the captain sat at his rotating command post, now dipping over Mexico, now swinging over Texas. Through his night binocs he surveyed a moveless world. Finally, Mayhem's voice came in on Charlie's radio. And just in time. Those batteries needed life breathed into them. And Mayhem was just the man to do it. He could breathe life into a dead bushwhacker.

"Apache Stalker! Apache Stalker! This is Geronimo Girolamo speaking. What is your position? Over."

"This is Stalker," Charlie shouted into the weak batteries. "Alien intruders are headed north by east toward Dryden. Over."

"Stalker! Stalker! Don't give me information until I request it . . . Now I'm requesting it. Which way are aliens headed? Over."

"North by east. Very fast. About a hundred of them. They must have slipped through your fingers. Over."

"Stalker! Stalker! Don't tell me what to do with my fingers! And don't give me numbers. If I want numbers, I'll ask for numbers. Now I'm asking. How many aliens have slipped through my fingers? Over."

"Two hundred and over. Over."

"I distinctly heard you say one hundred. Over."

"Another wave has just come over the border. Over."

"Zacotans or Zobracans? Over."

"Both. Over."

"Over what? Over."

"Over the river. Over," Charlie shouted.

"Good work, Stalker. I'll see that you get some extra pay for this. We'll seal off the road to Dryden. I'll send my best Bushmen—the kickers and whackers—what I call the elite . . . O-o-oops!" There was a creak, a crash, a splash. "Hydraulic line broke. *Sabotage!*" Captain Girolamo K. Mayhem's voice could be heard descending into water, gurgling a little.

"Good work, Charlie," the troops said. Another victory.

"We bought some time," Charlie said. "They'll come back down on us later. Now we head northwest toward Sanderson." He looked around him. "Where's Marvin?"

"I think he followed the dogs," Tiffany said.

"That kid's got to stop doin' that," Slam Dunk said. "Someday he won't make it back."

But little Marvin made it back. He came in smiling, and the dogs came in licking their lips.

"Loosen up!" Charlie commanded.

"Loosen up!" Dirk echoed.

"Slow and easy at the first," Charlie said.

"Slow and easy at the first," said Dirk.

"Head out," Charlie said, moving up the trail.

"Head out," Dirk said, moving in behind him.

"Shut up, Dirk," Charlie said.

"Shut up, Dirk," Dirk said.

They moved out in a slow trot, north by west toward Sanderson.

On and on. Into the night. One foot after the other. Soft sounds of padding moccasins, sniffling noses, hoarse breathing, and heavy grunting. They might have been Apaches, stealing through the darkness to their mountain retreat. Certainly no Apache ever ran with more dedication. And certainly no Apache ever grunted out his weariness with more sincerity.

Charlie pushed the wobbly little Indians five more miles. "Only thirty more to go," he said, winding everybody down. He didn't have to wind far.

"Don't think we can make it nonstop," Marvin said, in a faint voice.

"My head's doin' funny things," Dirty Little Harry said. He was breathing like a tired horse.

"Can we flop now, Charlie?" Dirk asked.

"If you flop now," Charlie said, "you'll never get up. First we've got to dig in. Put up the wickiups."

"I don't think I brought a wickiup," Dirk said. "What does it look like?"

"It looks like a brush pile," Charlie said. "In fact, it is a brush pile. The only thing is, it's empty in the middle. That's where you flop."

"I'll flop anywhere," Dirk said.

Charlie was good at wickiups. "Here's the trick," he told his weary braves, gathering up an armload of brushy limbs. "You weave the brush together. Bent limbs work best. It's just a big bird cage stuck in the sand. Nothing to it, really. The important thing is to plant the wickiup in the terrain so it can't be seen. And always put the wickiups in a circle on a small rise. That way, you don't have to worry about intruders."

"How about snakes?" Tiffany asked.

"Stomp 'em to death," Dirty Little Harry said.

"How big is a wickiup?" Marvin asked.

"All sizes," Charlie said. "Small, medium, and large."

"Are the dogs inside or out?"

"In the middle," Charlie said, "with the wickiups around them."

"That way," Slam Dunk said, "if they see a rabbit or anything, they alert us by tearing down the wickiups as they attack."

"Works every time," Charlie said.

Nothing like taking your work seriously. The funny thing about wickiups was, it didn't matter whether you built them seriously or not. They came out about the same. Just the thing a hard-pressed vagrant like Charlie would take to his heart. One of the best temporary—very temporary— dwellings ever built. Kept off the sun. Air-conditioned, too. Pure air, at that. At night, you could peep through the rafters and do your homework on the stars. Fortunately, it didn't rain too much in that part of the world; otherwise, you might have experienced some discomfort. But the most beautiful thing about the wickiup was, it blended with the earth—safe from prying eyes.

And a good thing it was, too. Come morning—which was now not far away—there would be many prying eyes about. When it came to tracking down fugitives, Captain Girolamo K. Mayhem's prying eyes never slept. Nor, for that matter, did Awful Ivan Hoffenhoff's imagination. As for Bugsy and Mugsy, they would pry into and under every bush in Texas for their suitcase. And then there were the prying eyes of Ellsworth Higgins Flake the Snitch, not to mention those of Grim Sam Stitcher the notorious tax collector. With all those prying eyes about, you had better build your wickiup in the right place.

And you had better be ready to run as well.

"Now," said Charlie, when they had finished the wick-iups, "we do the foot ceremony."

"Is that something religious?" Tiffany asked.

"Where you burn incense?" asked Slam Dunk.

"And light candles?" Marvin asked.

"Actually, it's a bedtime ceremony," Charlie said. "Chapter 2 in the manual. Very simple. Works wonders for the feet—and the spirit. You can neglect food and drink," he said, warming to his subject, "but you can't neglect your feet. Slip off your Smokin' Hopis and wet your fingers from your canteen. Now clean between your toes. Don't bother with the rest of your foot."

"Speaking of food—" Slam Dunk said.

"Don't speak of it," Charlie interrupted.

"How about a cracker?" Dirk asked. "With maybe a little of that green cheese?"

"Okay," Charlie said. "No reason why we can't eat and clean our toes at the same time. Might be interesting. Better sniff that Spam."

"See if the dogs will eat it," Dirty Little Harry suggested.

The dogs snapped it up.

"Then it's okay," Little Harry said, snapping up what the dogs left.

"Break out the bread," Slam Dunk said. "And the hammers and saws."

What started then was the foot ceremony, accompanied by dribbles of water between toes, bread crusts scattered on the ground, and hungry dogs straddling the group.

"If you smear a little Spam on your toes, the dogs will lick 'em clean," Marvin said. "Saves water."

Ingenious.

It was a combination banquet and dog show. In the darkness, nobody could see exactly what they were eating. But finally they got it all together and both food and foot ceremonies were going at the same time.

"First," Charlie said, "pop your toes, loud and clear."

The sounds were clear but not loud, being muffled by damp chunks of bread and cheese in the hands that did the popping.

"Sure a messy ceremony," Tiffany said.

"Now," said Charlie, "here's the important part." From a pocket of his Sweet Life Survival Pants he extracted a handful of marbles. "Don't lose 'em," he said. "They're valuable." He tossed the marbles on the ground in the ceremonial circle. "Pick 'em up, one by one, with your toes. Pick one up. Drop it. Pick another up."

Now they were smacking and picking and pushing off the dogs—who wanted to play with the marbles—at the same time.

"They slip," said Dirk.

"That's because your toes are greasy," Marvin said.

"Wipe 'em off with the bread," said Little Harry.

"Keep pickin'," Charlie said. Charlie was pickin' too. He was good at it, though he had always believed that dealing cards with your toes was actually a better exercise. "Now," he said after a time, "for the next part of the ceremony." He looked around him. "We need a Coke bottle." A Coke bottle in the middle of the desert. Well, it could happen. But he settled for some short stumps of wood he found on the ground. "Roll your arches over them," he said. "Back and forth."

"And pick up the marbles at the same time?" Slam Dunk asked.

"You can leave off with the marbles. Now we're goin' to work on the metatarsal."

"I think a dog swallowed a marble," Marvin said.

"What's a metatarsal?" Tiffany asked.

"That's the big arch in your foot. The one that gives you the bounce. It's your secret weapon. You can't run without one."

"I didn't know that," Marvin marveled. "Good thing you told us."

"Anybody got any knee trouble?" Charlie asked. "I got a knee ceremony, too."

"*No knee trouble*," they all assured him at once.

"Good knees."

"Strong knees."

"The best knees."

"Prize knees."

"They bend like crazy."

If there was one thing they didn't need, it was another ceremony. All they needed was sleep.

"Okay. Take over, Dirk," Charlie said to his unofficial trainer. "Run through the ceremony one more time."

And Dirk took over. They rolled their arches, picked up more marbles, popped more toes, ate more food, and finally—as the first light of day began to arrive—leaned back against their wickiups. The foot ceremony was over.

Sleep came easily after that. All they had to do was flop. The two luckier ones—Dirk and Dirty Harry—even managed to get a dog under their heads.

High noon. A blazing sun. The runners awoke. Refreshed.
Nothing like a good night's sleep in a wickiup. The spirits
were up.

And so were Captain Mayhem's helicopters, all two of
them. They were what he called his Strategic Air Command.
The Sagebrush Patrol would have been a better name.

But Captain Mayhem's helicopters couldn't find the wickiups. They might as well have been searching for a single
sagebrush in a sea of sagebrush. They did put on a good
show, though. Just what the fugitives needed to take their

minds off the heat, which, according to their Sweet Life thermometers, was 112°. That was inside the wickiups. Outside, it was closer to what you call fatal. Fortunately, they had their Arabian head shawls; otherwise, there might have been mass sunstroke. The Afghans looked as if they had something worse than that. They weren't designed for that kind of heat. No one—man or beast—was designed for that kind of heat. No one, that is, except Captain Girolamo K. Mayhem and Awful Ivan Hoffenhoff. That was because the sun had got them both for good long ago. Heat or no heat, sun or no sun, they just kept coming. And now, having been tricked the night before, they were coming with a vengeance.

Charlie and his Apaches watched from their wickiups. The unfolding show was distant but clear—widescreen video. Pennants, which were supposed to be flying, were drooping in the heat. Bodies, awaiting medics, were littered over the sand. Already, very high up, the older and wiser buzzards were circling. Once, late in the afternoon, a lone helicopter hovered directly over their heads, rattling and shaking the wickiups, but then it fluttered away, leaving them slightly cooler than before.

"We could have shot him down," Little Harry said, "if we'd had a cannon."

Mayhem's troops sortied out and sortied back in the blazing heat, leaving more bodies draped over the bushes. Ambulances, trying to reach them, mired down in the soft sand, grinding their wheels until they disappeared. And still the buzzards circled.

"Wonder what their strategy is?" Slam Dunk asked.

"Looks like it's just attack and keep on attacking," Charlie said. "The border patrol has an endless supply of bodies. Let's try the radio. We may as well have a little audio to go with the picture. Also, we might learn something." He poked a button. The batteries had grown weaker. The heat was probably getting them, too.

"I'm thirsty," Tiffany said. The heat was getting Tiffany as well.

"It was the crackers," Slam Dunk said.

"How many dribbles can we have, Charlie?" Tiffany asked.

"Two dribbles," Charlie said, still poking at the radio. "And a dribble for the dogs."

Tiffany shared her dribbles with the dogs. Then she patted their heads with her wet hands.

"Maybe we can find that horse tank tonight, huh?" Marvin said.

The thought was cooling.

Finally, Charlie poked the right button. *"Gather up the bodies,"* the radio blared. *"We're movin' out."* Old Mayhem sure had a way of bringing up the voltage. But the batteries had a way of fading out. Mayhem's voice disappeared.

"Now, let's see which way they start moving," Charlie said. "It's my guess that they plan to cut us off at Blacktop 90 tonight."

"Last Stand at Blacktop 90," Dirk said.

"More like Turnabout at Blacktop 90," Slam Dunk said, "if it goes like the last time."

"Say again," said Charlie, doing a surprised turnabout of his own. "You been here before?"

"Lots of times," Slam Dunk said. "They caught us every time. On Blacktop 90. The truck always broke down."

"They spread-eagled us," Marvin said.

"Shook us down," Dirk added.

"Then put us in another truck and took us back," Tiffany said. "We had to stand before the judge."

"And promise never to do it again," Marvin said.

"Blacktop 90's called the Road to Nowhere," Slam Dunk said. "We been goin' up and down it for as long as I can remember."

"How'd you think we learned English so good?" Dirty Little Harry asked.

"Television," Charlie said. "How else?"

"Only partly," Little Harry said. "We learned it from Clint Eastwood and Burt Reynolds and Blacktop 90. You learn fast on Blacktop 90."

"That's the road the Gone-Forever Mack took," Dirk said.

"It probably broke down again," Dirty Harry said.

Nothing about his troops could surprise Charlie now. When it came to running for survival, they were real sweet-lifers. Reminded him of his favorite song. The blacktops and the junkyards and the wheat fields and the clothes-lines. He kept poking the radio, trying to get the right wavelength. Finally, he got it. Captain Mayhem was noisily giving orders to his Strategic Air Command—code-named Geese.

"Goose One! Goose Two! This is Gander calling. Have you sighted goslings? Report to me at Gaggle Base. Over."

On the flimsy radio, Mayhem sounded like a gander. And the geese like a gaggle. Squawks. Honks. Hisses. It was goose heaven.

"Gander! Gander! This is Goose One. No sight of goslings. Returning to Gaggle Base. Over."

"Goose One! Goose Two! I'll tell you when to return to

Gaggle Base when I'm ready for you to return to Gaggle Base. Keep scouring the bushes for goslings. Over."

"Gander! Gander! This is Goose One. We are low on goose juice. In fact, we're out of goose juice."

"That's a funny name for gas," Slam Dunk said.

"Code," Dirty Little Harry explained.

Mayhem hissed back. "I'll tell you when you're out of goose juice when I'm ready to tell you. Now I'm ready. You are out of goose juice. Return to Gaggle Base. Out."

Charlie poked a button. "Gander! Gander!" he said. "This is Super Goose. Over."

"Who the—!" Gander sounded as if he had been strangled. "Stand by! Stand by! Identify yourself, Super Goose. Over."

"This is GASH," Charlie said. "Gaggle Allied Supreme Headquarters. And I am Super Goose. What are your plans for the night attack? Over."

"Super Goose! Super Goose!" Gander replied, before such high authority. "We swoop down and cut 'em off at Blacktop 90 tonight. Over."

"Make sure you do," Super Goose Charlie said. "Otherwise, I'll have your head. Out."

The goslings applauded. The dogs looked puzzled.

"That's it," Charlie said. "Blacktop 90."

The words had an ominous sound. Blacktop 90 was the enemy. That unbeatable road had to be beaten. One more defeat and they would be permanent Blacktop 90 dropouts. What it really came down to was Showdown at Blacktop 90, where things had to be decided once and for all. Slowly, as the sun dropped, their determination rose.

"We'll cross it at midnight," Charlie said, "when the kickers and whackers will be seeing shadows."

"And maybe dead drunk," Marvin said.

"They were the last time," Tiffany said.

"It's a ten-mile run to the road," Charlie continued. "We'll do it in two heats."

"Then we hit trouble, right?" Dirk asked.

"Right," said Charlie. "All kinds of trouble."

They had already hit trouble. They just didn't know it yet. It was the Afghans who sounded the alarm. Their ears came up, their noses after them. Then they started growling low.

"We got visitors," Slam Dunk said.

"Friendly or otherwise?" Marvin asked.

"Otherwise," said Slam Dunk.

"Keep down," Charlie warned. "And hold the dogs."

Tiffany held the dogs, one arm around each.

Charlie peeped out of the wickiup, five other peepers and two dogs over his shoulder. Slam Dunk pointed. "There they are," he said. About two hundred yards away, coming up a dry streambed, were Bugsy and Mugsy—the Tex-Mex Connection. They were guided by Ellsworth Higgins Flake the Snitch.

"Just what we needed," Charlie said. "Stand by for action."

"We've got to work fast," Dirk said.

"That's right," Marvin agreed. "What do we do?"

"What would you do?" Charlie asked Marvin.

"I'd take 'em in a trap," Marvin said.

"Yeah," Dirk said, "an Apache trap. We bury ourselves in the sand—head and all. Then we jump up . . . "

"And pump 'em full of . . . " Dirty Harry hesitated.

"Full of what?" Tiffany asked.

"Anything we can find," Dirty Little Harry said.

"We better do somethin'," Slam Dunk said. "Or they're gonna pump us full of somethin'."

"Okay," Charlie said. "Get your Sweet Life Survival Shovels out of your Bloomie Bags. Then start diggin'. Dig wide and deep, right in front of the wickiups. Right there." He pointed. "Do you see my plan?"

"We dig you," Slam Dunk said. "Put the trap in the middle of the trail."

"That's right," Charlie said. "When they come in close, they'll see only the wickiups. One-track minds."

"We dig you, we dig you," the diggers said impatiently. "They stumble into the hole."

"And we cover 'em over," Marvin said.

"And put up a cross to mark the grave," said Dirty Little Harry.

"More or less," Charlie said. "But leave their feet sticking up if you can. It's their wedgies we want. That will demobilize 'em."

"The Stalker's not wearin' wedgies," Slam Dunk said, digging furiously.

"We'll take whatever we can get," Charlie said. "Just keep out of the way of that musket. And watch the other two. They don't fight fair."

Tiffany was having trouble holding the dogs. They had caught the Stalker's scent—promising blood.

"Take them on ahead," Charlie told her, "and hide behind a rock."

"I wanta watch the burial," she said.

"You can watch it from a distance. Just keep the dogs quiet until we get the victims in the hole. Then turn them loose."

Sand was flying in all directions now.

"They're only about a hundred yards away," Charlie said, peeping over a rock.

"Dig!" Slam Dunk ordered.

They dug. More sand flew. Sometimes the sand rolled back faster than they could dig it out. But they kept on digging. Marvin and Dirk and Harry were dropping slowly from sight. Only Slam Dunk's head could be seen. Finally, they got it deep enough, and maybe wide enough, too. "Just enough to squeeze 'em in," Slam Dunk said. Charlie reached down and pulled them up, one by one.

"Get behind the rocks," he said, "and make yourselves invisible."

Nothing to it. They had been making themselves invisible all their lives. By the rivers and the sagebrush and the windmills and the canyons.

Carefully, Charlie laid some branches over the hole, scattering dead leaves and twigs across them. Then he brushed out the surrounding sand to give it a natural look. It might not have fooled a pure Apache, but it would fool an impure one like Ellsworth, and even more impure ones like Bugsy and Mugsy.

"Just in time," he whispered, sliding behind the rocks. "If Tiff can hold the dogs."

"And we can hold our breath," Slam Dunk said.

All of them were puffing like locomotives.

Charlie raised his hand for silence. Bugsy and Mugsy had left the ravine and were hobbling up the hill on their open-toed wedgies with the cork soles. It was painful to watch. Ellsworth the Stalker seemed disinclined to get any closer. Maybe he did have a touch of Apache in him. About twenty feet before they got to the hole, Ellsworth pointed at the circle of wickiups and said, "There they are. Pay me."

"I don't see anybody," the twins muttered at the same time.

"They're inside the huts," the Stalker said. "Asleep. Only insane people go out in this heat. Pay me."

"First the bodies," Bugsy said. "Then the money."

"Yeah," said Mugsy. "First the merchandise. We wanta see a few arms and legs flyin' around."

"I think I heard a dog," Bugsy said. "Did you hear a dog, Mugsy?"

"I heard somethin'. Thought it was my feet protestin'. These wedgies are murder."

"There's a suitcase full of money in there," Bugsy reminded him.

"Pay me," the Stalker kept saying.

"We can't," Bugsy said, "until we get the suitcase."

"Yeah," said Mugsy. "First the suitcase and then the money."

"First the money," the Stalker said.

It was another standoff.

Finally, the Tex-Mex twins screwed up their courage and limped carefully toward the wickiups. On tiptoe, in high-heeled wedgies, they looked like two upright pigs doing a slow toe dance.

Tippy-toe. Tippy-toe.

Then came the *crash*, and Bugsy and Mugsy went head over wedgies into the grave. Looking up, seeing the head shawls, they screamed, "A-rabs! A-rabs! Good Lord, they're A-rabs!"

"Turn the dogs loose!" Charlie shouted to Tiff.

Tiff had already turned the dogs loose. Seeing them, Ellsworth Higgins Flake the Apache Stalker split.

"A-rabs! A-rabs!" screamed the Tex-Mex twins.

"Get the wedgies!" Charlie shouted.

"Cover 'em up," Dirty Harry shouted, shoveling like crazy.

"I can't find their feet," Slam Dunk shouted.

Everybody was shouting and shoveling.

"Their feet are down here," Marvin shouted from below. Marvin had fallen into the hole. Dirty Harry was covering him, too.

"You're burying him alive," Dirk shouted to Dirty Harry.

Up flew a wedgie through a cloud of sand. Down below, Marvin was wrestling with feet and sand at the same time. Up came another wedgie. Then Slam Dunk saw a pair of feet sticking straight up in the air. Off came the wedgies.

"Cover 'em up! Cover 'em up!" Little Harry shouted. The kid had gone crazy.

"Where's Dirk?" Charlie asked.

"Down here!" Dirk shouted from below. "Helpin' Marvin."

"Cover 'em up! Cover 'em up!" There was no stopping Dirty Little Harry. He had become a demon shoveler.

"Owww!" Dirk cried from below. "Somebody bit me!"

"Bite him back," Slam Dunk shouted, trying to uncover Dirk and Marvin.

"He didn't bite your foot, did he?" Charlie asked, aghast at the possibility.

"No. He bit my ear," Dirk shouted.

"Well, that's okay," Charlie said.

"Hang on," Slam Dunk shouted to Dirk. "I've got you by the hair."

Slam Dunk pulled him up. Actually, he pulled both of them up, since Marvin also had Dirk by the hair.

"Now," Slam Dunk said to Dirty Little Harry, "shovel to your heart's content."

Down the trail, almost out of sight, the Apache Stalker was running for his life, the dogs nipping at his heels. Now and then you could hear a yelp, and now and then some more human sound.

"Good work," Charlie said, when they had finally got Little Harry under control. "By the time they get out, we'll be halfway to Blacktop 90. And they'll be shoeless."

"I think I hear 'em gruntin'," Marvin said, laying his ear on the mound.

"They do that good," Dirk said.

The dogs came back in. They seemed to have smiles on their faces.

"They've got blood on their noses," Dirk said.

"You've got blood on your ear," Tiffany said.

"I got blood all over me," said Marvin.

The battle was over. All they had to do was treat the wounded. They got out their Sweet Life Medical Kits and patched up their ears and other tender spots. Then they shook the sand from their Smokin' Hopis, popped and snapped their toes, wiggled their ankles, and cleaned out the holes in their noses to let in all the air they could get. Maximum oxygen intake, Charlie called it.

The sun was just going down when they set out on a slow jog north. By the time the sun disappeared, they were floating through the night-sweet air over the dark terrain. And a little after that, they were streaming.

Bring on your Blacktop 90, world.

Here the mood of the runners changed. Now it was sheer determination. The closer they got to Blacktop 90, the more grimly they ran. Even the Afghans seemed to sense some change of spirit in these complicated human games. It was as if the words "Blacktop 90" had changed the music. Instead of bells and flügelhorns, they now heard distant choirs telling them to beat the unbeatable road and cross the uncrossable line—and, in the end, to run the impossible run.

Five miles from that unbeatable road, they came slowly

to a halt, running in place silently. Silently, too, they eased their lungs, dribbled water on their lips, wobbled a little until their strength came back, and then walked slowly about in the soft sand. No one had to tell them now how to relax. And besides, no one had any breath to waste.

There was no horseplay. Nor was there any boasting. They knew from experience that you didn't joke or brag about your exploits on Blacktop 90. Blacktop 90 was a road that took your assaults, brought your dreams crashing down, and then perhaps—who knows?—grieved awhile for you. You had to respect a road like that.

After a time, Charlie asked, "Anybody sick at the stomach?"

"A little bit," Dirty Harry said. A rare confession from him.

"Me, too," said Dirk.

"That's natural," Charlie said. "It'll pass. Splash a little water on your face."

Tiffany took the opportunity to splash some on the dogs.

"Pop your knees," Charlie said. "And while you're at it, shake out your metatarsals. Then do a few swings to relax your spine." Charlie knew what it took to cross the uncrossable line. He wanted every little edge the human body could supply. "Now," he said, while they popped and swung, "here's the plan. It's called the Two-Wave Assault. Listen closely. About fifty yards from Blacktop 90, we take cover in the brush. Then we locate the kickers and whackers, hoping they don't locate us first. After that, we time the patrol cars as they pass. And don't forget, they'll be cruising up and down from two directions, some with lights on, some with lights off. Old Mayhem will probably have a thousand troops up and down that road all night. And you never know where Awful Ivan and his slow-witted deputy will be. The long claws of the law are out." Charlie paused. The kids waited. "Now, here's the important part. When a patrol car passes, three of you will slide across the road in back of it. That's the first wave. Go low and go fast. When the next patrol car passes, the remaining three of us will go. That's the second wave. Once the first three are across, keep on runnin' straight ahead."

"How far?" someone asked.

"Till you drop," Charlie said. "That's the danger zone, the moment of life and death. The second three will be comin' on behind you. When they catch you, ease up and start floatin' north."

"Suppose the second wave doesn't catch the first wave?"

"It will."

"Suppose we get separated?"

"I've thought of that, too," Charlie said. "That's where the dogs come in. The first wave will take a dog. The second wave will keep a dog behind. No matter where you go, the dogs will find each other."

"Sounds good to me," Marvin said. "Who goes first?"

"I've got that worked out, too," Charlie said. "Scientifically, I might add. It's a known fact that long legs have a better chance of catching short legs than the other way around."

"What does that mean?" Dirk asked.

"It means that the first to cross will be Dirk the Turk, Dirty Little Harry, and Marvin Lee, in that order. One, two, three."

Astonishment rippled over the group. Pride rippled over the younger three.

Leaders!

"There's only one thing wrong with that," Dirk said.

"What's that?"

"If I'm leadin', the others might have trouble keepin' up."

"Just keep out of our way," Marvin said to Dirk.

"We'll probably pass you," Dirty Harry said.

It so pleased the three little musketeers to be the first wave that they never even noticed that they had not exactly been chosen for their blazing speed.

"That leaves Tiffany, Slam Dunk, and me," Charlie said, "in that order. One, two, three. Don't look back to see if we're comin'. Just keep goin' wide open. I mean *wide* open."

"Don't worry about that," said Dirk.

"If anything goes wrong . . . " Charlie hesitated.

Marvin interrupted him. "What could go wrong?"

"Someone could get caught," Tiffany said.

"Or shot," said Dirty Little Harry.

"Or bust a leg," Dirk said.

When it came to things going wrong, each had his private fear. This was, after all, Blacktop 90. Charlie was sorry he had mentioned it. "Maybe Marvin's right," he said. "Nothing will go wrong. Now, that about covers it. Any questions?"

All the questions had been asked. "Lead out, Dirk," Charlie said. "You may as well get a little practice before the big run."

"Right on," said Dirk. "Gather round." That little guy really did like to give orders. "We do the first mile in a long jog. Then we pick up and float for the second mile, keepin' loose. After that, we start streamin'. Keep your eye on me and keep close. No stragglers. By the time we reach the road, we'll probably be doin' a slow and easy stumble."

Which was, more or less, the way they did it. Maybe Dirk's long jog wasn't as long as it might have been, and his slow and easy stumble came more quickly than it should have, but no great matter. Dirk had a dog up front, and Charlie had a dog at the back. The dogs seemed to be rising and falling in the same place. At times, in the deeper sand, Dirk seemed to be doing the same. But there were no comments from the others. Little Dirk was the leader, giving it his all. In his mind, he no doubt thought that he was floating and streaming. He may even have thought that he was flying. Judging by the sound of his grunting, he was probably convinced that he was breaking records. One thing was certain: he was determined.

By the time they hit the four-mile point, determination was about the only thing Dirk had left. If a breeze had come out of the north, he might have started going backwards. But he kept on stumbling, one foot after the other, until at last they could see the flashing lights of patrol cars up and down Blacktop 90. At a safe distance from the road, Dirk reduced his efforts until he and the others were running in place. You could hardly tell the difference.

"Slow and easy," Dirk panted, half dead. "Slow and easy. Don't want anybody dropping on me now." Put that way, you had a feeling the little Turk could have grunted and stumbled another mile.

Now they peered through the darkness at the fateful road. And the odds, it was clear, favored Blacktop 90. More than a black and lonely ribbon through the sagebrush, it looked like a racetrack or a circus. Lights, lights, lights. Red lights, green lights, yellow lights, all of them flashing. Captain Girolamo K. Mayhem had his forces out in full—and, as it turned out, a few others to boot. Taking no chances.

"Look at that!" Marvin Lee marveled. "It looks like El Paso."

"You been to El Paso, too?" Charlie asked.

"Yeah. We tried it that way once. Got caught there, too. Except that was Four Lane 80."

"Truck broke down, eh?"

"Ran out of gas."

"And the Coyote driver ran off with our money," Little Harry said.

Lights and more lights. "Don't look directly at them," Charlie cautioned. "It'll ruin your night vision."

"How do you keep from it?" Slam Dunk asked. "They're everywhere."

"Watch the stars," Charlie said, "and keep blinking. Keeps the eyes soft."

"You mean those stars on the side of the patrol cars?"

"What stars?" Charlie asked. "Mayhem's vehicles don't have stars."

Charlie looked. Then he jumped. "Texas Rangers!"

"What are they doin' here?" Tiffany asked. "I thought just the feds were supposed to chase us."

"Mayhem probably called for a backup," Charlie said. "If so, he sure called the right bunch. When it comes to playin' games, those guys go at it like football players. Keep low. They don't know where we are, but any minute now they'll start actin' as if they do."

They crowded in under the bushes and the rocks.

"Where's the crazy captain?" Slam Dunk asked.

"There he is!" Tiffany pointed.

And there he was, in all his glory. You could hardly miss him. At his command post high atop a truck, seated in a swivel chair, his maps laid out before him, his night binocs in one hand and a loudspeaker in the other, he was cruising majestically and slowly along the road. Seeing him like

that, so kingly in the night, you half expected the lowly kickers and whackers to run up and bow and throw thistles at his feet.

"This is Top Dog! This is Top Dog!" he boomed through the bullhorn. "You are surrounded. Throw down your poison darts."

Then a little confusion broke out atop the truck. After what seemed a brief and vicious struggle for the bullhorn, Awful Ivan Hoffenhoff's voice came booming through. "Aliens! Intruders! Put down your knives and crawl to the middle of the road, with your hands up."

"I'd like to see somebody do that," Marvin Lee said.

More sounds of struggle for possession of the bullhorn. Squeaks. Squawks. A muffled "Give me that thing, you old idiot!" and then another voice from the command post: "This is Ranger Kammerlock speaking. You are in violation of the laws of Texas. Come out or be destroyed."

"Who's he?" someone asked.

"That's Diehard Kammerlock," Charlie said. "The oldest Ranger in Texas. Refuses to die until he cleans up the border. Been at it now for sixty years."

All kinds of noises were coming from the loudspeaker now. It sounded as if the three commanders were slugging it out for control. "Gimme that horn! Gimme that horn!"

"I'm bettin' on Diehard Kammerlock," Slam Dunk said. "With a name like that, you can't lose."

"Keep low," Charlie said. "The kickers and whackers are goin' on foot patrol."

"Are you sure they don't know where we are?" Tiffany asked.

"Positive," Charlie said.

It looked for a moment as if Charlie might be wrong. Patrol cars kept converging. Kickers and whackers were kicking and whacking all around them. You could hear their big gruff voices talking about what a beautiful night it was for kickin' and whackin', and how they must have kicked and whacked every bush along that road at least a hundred times in the last six months.

"You can tell they love their work," Slam Dunk said.

From the command post high atop the truck, Captain Mayhem had temporarily gained control. "Break out the flares!" he ordered, standing up on his swivel chair, waving his night binocs in all directions.

Another struggle broke out for the loudspeaker. "Gimme that thing," Diehard Kammerlock roared. "Don't fire the flares! Don't fire the flares! You'll burn up Texas!"

"*Flares!*" cried Mayhem, seizing the horn again. "Fire the flares!"

Someone fired a flare, just in time to give the huddled fugitives a view of Awful Ivan struggling to get the bullhorn away from Diehard Kammerlock, who had seized it from Mayhem. But that was the last they saw of Awful Ivan for a while. In his struggle for supreme command, he made the mistake of pouncing on Diehard Kammerlock. Unfortunately for him, he missed, sailing off the back of the truck into the brush below. There, awaiting him, was Halfway Hebe, turning about in circles, lost as usual.

"More flares!" Mayhem cried, in full control now. "Oops!" His maps went flying into space.

Someone shot another flare, then another, then a barrage. The night was bright as day. Also the sagebrush was burning.

"I told you!" Diehard Kammerlock screamed hoarsely. "You crazy old arsonist. Now you've got yourself a prairie fire."

"Flares!" cried Mayhem. "More flares."

More flares rose into the night.

"This is gettin' serious," Slam Dunk said. "The whole county's on fire."

"Keep cool. Keep cool," Charlie said. "If worse comes to worst, we can always retreat."

That unbeatable road
That uncrossable line

"We *can't* retreat," Marvin Lee said. There was desperation in his voice. "This time we've got to make it."

"Marvin's right," Dirk said. "If that road beats us again, we might . . . "

" . . . Turn to a life of crime," Dirty Little Harry finished. "Or something worse."

"It was just a thought," Charlie said. "Temporary retreat. One way or another, we'll make it."

The truth was, there wasn't one way, or another either. Fires now crackled around them. They were caught in a trap. It was too much to hope that Mayhem's gas tank might explode. The flares had all been shot away from the trucks, and there wasn't enough wind to blow the flames in any direction. Everything was burning, but it was burning straight up.

That was when the heavy smoke began to get the fugitives. It was an ugly sight hanging in the air—white, low, and thick, like fog. Charlie shuddered to think what that would do to your lungs, particularly lungs that were already raw from running. But then he saw that the smoke was the only friend they had in that eerie melee. "Change of plans," he whispered to the troops. "Dig out those cloth masks from the survival kits, and dampen them with water."

They dug frantically, the dogs huddled close around them. It took only a minute. With the masks on, and the Arabian head shawls, their faces were barely visible.

"More flares!" cried Mayhem, who was holding Diehard Kammerlock down with one hand and the bullhorn with the other. "Fire at will."

"Now," said Charlie, "listen carefully. We're goin' for it through the smoke. As soon as those two coughing bushwhackers out there get out of our way, we head straight for the back of the command truck. It'll be a one-wave assault instead of a two-wave assault. And don't lose sight of the person ahead of you. Clear?"

"Clear."

"Who leads?" asked Dirk.

"You do," said Charlie. "Same order as before. The only difference is, we sprint through the smoke and never look back." Charlie paused. Then he said, "Now, little earthlings, it's after-burner time. I guess you know that."

"We know that."

"Okay. Take your places."

They lined up, dogs and all. The two bushwhackers moved off away from their path. Then Charlie gave the order with civilized and traditional respect for the running game all over the earth. "On your marks. Get set. Go!"

They went.

And that was where, for sure, the comedy of that crazy night reached its highest point. For in their wild run to the back of the command truck, they ran smack up against Awful Ivan Hoffenhoff and Halfway Hebe. It was almost like running into a couple of trucks. Perhaps their speed saved them, or their agility, or maybe even their fright. But more likely it was their masks and the Arabian head shawls, showing only their frantic eyes. Seeing such a sight, such eyes, Awful Ivan stood petrified, unable even to pounce. The best he could do was to drop to his knees and cry in a hoarse voice, "Forgive me, Lord. I have sinned." Of course, the guttural sound which Dirk the Turk made as he plunged headlong into Awful Ivan hadn't hurt either.

That was the first act. In the second act, they plunged headlong into none other than the Apache Stalker. In that furious instant, the Stalker—sneaky and fast—snapped a tiny button to the bottom of a passing pant leg. And though they left him mangled in the cactus, they now carried with them a tiny electronic bug, silent to them, but beeping out their position regularly to Top Dog himself. It was a dirty but effective trick, and one that certainly threatened to bring them to grief later on.

But there was no grieving now. They were on the other side of the road, out of the smoke, tearing off the masks, the after-burners burning.

Don't cry for us, Blacktop 90.

11

"Rally 'round the flag, boys!" Top Dog roared through the bullhorn. His maps were flying in the breeze.

It was a beautiful scene, like some heroic painting held aloft by invisible hands. The burning sagebrush cast a glow over everything. Made you think of the dawn's early light, all the more so since the banner of the Jolly Bushmen was still waving. In the middle of the scene, smoke billowing around him, Captain Girolamo K. Mayhem stood on his swivel chair, turning in all directions, crying, "After them!"

The Jolly Bushmen and Headhunters roared off in their jeeps and patrol cars, only to mire down in the sand and come to a grinding halt.

"We need three-wheelers!" Top Dog shouted. "Where are the three-wheelers?"

"We need horses!" cried Diehard Kammerlock, over the horn. "To horse! To horse!"

"Horses are obsolete," Mayhem roared back.

Another wrestling match threatened to break out. In fact, it threatened to become a free-for-all, since Awful Ivan had climbed back up to the command post and was pursuing the swivel chair in its rotation. Top Dog was calling for jeeps and three-wheelers, Diehard was calling for horses, while Awful Ivan was calling for gorilla warfare complete with booby traps and flamethrowers.

Beautiful though the scene was, it was actually little more than smoke and noise. For Charlie and his fugitives had escaped into the night.

Dirk was still leading, which meant that they were going up and down a lot. It also meant that Dirk was grunting a lot. This had been the biggest night of the little fellow's life. His child's mind was spinning with thoughts of victory. Now, at last, all the blacktops and four-lanes were behind them, as were the broken-down trucks and the grim-faced Coyotes. Dirk the Leader. It sounded good. And it was true. He had led them across the uncrossable road. Through the smoke. Through Awful Ivan. Over the Apache Stalker. Through every peril the night had to offer. Then he stumbled on for five hard miles. Now he was leading them to Blanco Canyon Hideout—and, all of them hoped, reunion. The trouble was, Blanco Canyon was still fifteen miles away, and Dirk the Turk was done for. Lifting one awfully heavy arm, he slow-stumbled them to a halt. It was all he could do to keep from falling.

"Why'd you stop?" Dirty Little Harry asked, so out of breath you could hardly hear him.

"Yeah," said Marvin Lee. "I thought we were gonna go nonstop." His voice was even fainter than Harry's.

Dirk didn't reply, because Dirk didn't have any voice left. Or knees either. He was wobbling all over the place. So were they all. One more step forward and it would have been crumple-time.

"Maybe I overdid it," Dirk gasped. "My stomach's doin' funny things. I think I'm goin' to . . ." He opened his mouth to do it and did it.

"Me, too," said Marvin Lee, holding his stomach.

"Grit your teeth," said Little Harry. But Little Harry had his mouth open, too.

"We're safe now," Charlie said to Dirk. "All we need's a little rest. Only fifteen miles to go."

Aching lungs. Pounding ears. Wobbly legs. Charlie might as well have said Alaska.

"We ran fifteen miles," Charlie said, "in one night. That's good running."

All of them looked up, wobbling still as they tried to run in place, hoping, too, that they didn't spoil anything by what their uncontrollable stomachs were doing.

Wiping his mouth with the back of his hand, Marvin Lee said, "That was a nice thing to say, Charlie."

"Yeah," said Little Harry, "real nice."

"What did I say?" Charlie asked.

"It's more what you didn't say," Marvin said.

"Yeah," said Little Harry. "You didn't say, 'That's good runnin' . . . for kids.' "

"Or," said Tiffany, " 'for girls.' "

"Or," said Dirk, " 'for short-legged little guys that grunt.' You just said, 'That's good runnin'."

"It was good running," Charlie said.

"We weren't streamin'," Dirk said.

"Or floatin'," said Marvin Lee.

"Mostly we were just goin' up and down," Tiffany said.

"Maybe so," said Charlie. "But if you noticed closely, you were goin' up and down in the right direction. That happens a lot when you're running what true runners call the Impossible Run."

The Impossible Run.

Their heads, which had been hanging low, lifted. Something about the words caught their fancy. More importantly, the words pecked at their tired spirits. They had unwound now and were sitting on a knoll among the rocks. Every now and then, Dirk would lean over a rock and open his mouth. Then the others would follow. Far in back of them the sagebrush was still burning. Along Blacktop 90, the captain's forces had regrouped and were pulling out. Some went east, others went west. Charlie knew what they would do next. They would swing wide around them and try to cut them off at Blanco Canyon Pass.

The Impossible Run. The words stuck in their minds. They had a hint of beauty, desperation, casualties—just the right ingredients to restore the faith, and the imagination.

"You mean maybe it's our bones on the desert?" Dirty Little Harry asked.

"We just fall forward in the sand," Marvin Lee said. "And jerk a little."

The spirits were lifting.

"Impossible?" Slam Dunk asked Charlie.

"That's what they call it," Charlie said, "when the spirit says yes and the odds say no. You're not supposed to make it. It's a battle between the human spirit and the odds."

Not supposed to make it.

It all belonged to the heroic world of "death-defying leaps," "take off the blindfold, amigos," and last stands at all the passes the earth had to offer. The only way to live. The odds against you. The chips down. The legs wobbly. The stomach in revolt. It was beautiful.

"Let's eat," Charlie said, "if we've got anything left."

Down to the last crumb. The water running low. Which may have been for the best, right then. Their stomachs couldn't have taken much, at least not successfully. So they dribbled the water over their lips, swallowing occasionally, shared what little food they had with the dogs, who declined most of it, especially the cheese, and then leaned back against the rocks. A cool breeze had lifted off the desert, but they didn't notice, having fallen asleep. In fact, they didn't notice anything for the next few hours. And when they did, they couldn't quite believe it.

A helicopter—Goose One—was hovering over them.

"Hunker down!" Charlie cried. "Hunker down!"

They were trapped.

12

It was just beginning to grow light in the east. Against the rocks, where they huddled, it was still dark.

"Something's terribly wrong," Charlie said. "There's no way they could know where we are."

"And yet," Slam Dunk said, "there they are. What does that do to the odds?"

"They just ran out," Charlie said. "From here on in, we're operating on blind faith."

The helicopter, though it had located their general position, seemed to have trouble pinpointing the exact spot.

It circled, came back, circled again, and then moved off down the trail.

"Somebody's directing them," Charlie said. "We're being watched. It's probably the Apache Stalker. Doin' his dirty work, as usual."

But there was no indication that the Stalker was anywhere about. Even the Afghans gave no signs. One Afghan was sniffing curiously at Dirk's ankle, as if in search of a crumb. Dirk pushed him away. But the cold nose came back, shoving and prodding at the ankle. The dog started whimpering softly, the hair rising on his neck. He had caught the Stalker's scent on the electronic bug.

"What's wrong with that dog?" Tiffany asked. "Come here, big fellow."

"He's gone mad," Dirk said. "Wants my leg."

"He smells something," Slam Dunk said.

"And he doesn't like the smell," Charlie said.

"And whatever it is, it's on you," Tiffany said to Dirk. She leaned over and felt the cold nose. It was pressing against a flat metallic object no bigger than a button. "Hooked to your pant leg," she told Dirk. She started to yank it off.

"Wait," said Charlie. He took a small knife from his pocket, cut a neat hole in Dirk's Sweet Life Survival Pants, and held up the bug. "Straight out of the Dirty Tricks Department," he said. "And it came from the dirtiest trickster of them all, Ellsworth Higgins."

"I thought his name was Flake," someone said.

"Flake, Higgins, whatever," Charlie said. "It doesn't matter. We were bugged. They knew where we were all the time. What's worse, they know where we are right now."

"What do we do with it?" Tiffany asked.

"Destroy it," Slam Dunk suggested.

"Maybe we can use it to our advantage," Charlie said.

"You mean turn the tables?"

"More like turn the beepers," Charlie said.

The helicopter circled them again.

"You mean, we mislead them," Marvin Lee said, "off into the wastes?"

"Where they wander forever," said Little Harry, "crying 'Water! Water!' "

"Show a little mercy," Tiffany scolded.

"They're not showin' us any," Little Harry protested.

"Don't waste your strength talking," Charlie said. "Before this day is out, you'll need it all. Right now, we've got to throw the helicopter off our trail. The best way to do it is to leave the beeper here for him to home in on while we home in on Blanco Canyon." Charlie paused. "I suppose you know they've forced us to run by day. We don't have any choice. The sun will be murderous. We'll have to keep to the arroyos and the brush."

"How far?" someone asked.

"Till we're safe," Charlie said.

"That might be forever," Tiffany said.

"Bring on the buzzards," said Dirty Little Harry.

"This may be the hardest day of your life," Charlie said.

"I thought yesterday was," Marvin Lee said.

"All I'm hopin'," Charlie said, "is that we've got enough strength left when the time comes to make the Miracle Kick."

The heads lifted.

"What's the Miracle Kick?" Slam Dunk asked.

"It's the last superhuman effort to reach the finish line. Actually, it's just a kick. But when there's nothing left in you to kick, and you kick anyway, it's called a Miracle Kick."

"What if you kick," Marvin Lee asked, "and nothing happens?"

"You're done for," said Little Harry.

"Let's move out," Charlie said, "while at least the shadows are still on our side." He laid the bug on the topmost rock. "Keep low," he said, as they slithered beneath the brush and into a dry arroyo. Then, just to see how much strength the little runners had left, he set them on a slow jog north.

The bells had gone for good now. So had the flügelhorns. Now they were running on nothing but blind hope. And on something else which only Charlie Jones knew about— the Pure Grit Factor. It was something not mentioned in any manual. There were too many unknowns in the factor to make rules about it. Pure grit came when everything else had gone. It was like the Miracle Kick. You hoped it was there when you needed it. Right now, the little fugitives needed it badly.

Somehow they found it. Despite the boiling sun, they hung on for another five miles. Their minds weren't thinking now; they were just pounding, like their legs and their hearts. When finally they stopped, nobody even had the strength to wind down. Instead, trembling, they dropped. Certainly, no one had the strength to joke. At least, not at the first. A little later, after Charlie had looked closely at their eyes and found them as close to normal as could be expected, Marvin Lee managed to say, "You think we'll live?"

"Just don't stretch out," Charlie said. "It might be fatal."

"It might be worse," Dirk said, "if I don't."

"Keep out of the sun," Charlie said. "Use the brush. Use anything you can get under."

There was no building wickiups now. They had to save

what energy they had for surprises, which the race seemed full of lately. That ugly little bug had thrown them off their plan. It had spoiled the purity of their effort. So long as the race was even remotely fair, they could take it for the game of stamina and wits it was. But the bug had changed things. Mostly, it had changed their awareness of things. They were in danger of losing that one important thing all true runners need: a total disregard for reality. You could not disregard the sun, without paying the price. Nor could your pure grit deny the fact that your muscles no longer obeyed you.

There are sweet moments in a runner's life, but this wasn't one of them.

"Dribble a little water on your lips," Charlie said.

"I'm almost out," Slam Dunk said.

"We all are," Tiffany said.

At the merest hint of water, the dogs came up licking. Tiffany let them lick her fingers as she dribbled a little on her face. Then she shook her Sweet Life Canteen. It barely made a noise.

Dirty Little Harry tried his canteen, but nothing came out. "You know what that means, don't you?" he said to Dirk.

"Sure," said the Turk. "It means your lips start crackin' and your tongue starts swellin'."

"And slobbers come out of your mouth," Marvin Lee added. "You also see visions."

"You call it Belly-Up Time," Little Harry explained.

There was, Charlie noticed, still a lingering disregard for reality—maybe just enough.

"Actually," Charlie said, "the manual calls it the Total Collapse Factor. Comes right after the Crazy-in-the-Head

Factor. But before that, you've got to go through the Pure Grit Factor."

"When do we go through that?" Marvin Lee asked.

"We're in the middle of it now," Charlie said.

"I think I'm in that other one," Dirk said. "I keep hearin' music."

"What kind of music?" Slam Dunk asked.

"Pretty music," said the Turk. "It's a waltz. Maybe it's a funeral waltz."

"You're crazy in the head, all right," Tiffany said.

"I hear guitars," Dirty Little Harry said. "And steel-drum bands."

"I hear angels singing," Marvin Lee said. "That's a sure sign . . ."

"That's a sure sign you're all crazy," Tiffany said.

But if they were crazy in the head, so were the Afghans, who lifted their noses and started whining softly. Then everybody knew that they were all either crazy in the head or really hearing music—for all of them could hear it now. It was growing louder, in the distance, approaching slowly.

"Is this the way it happens, Charlie?" Dirk asked. "Madness, I mean."

"Let's have a look," Charlie said.

They slipped up to the high rocks on the ridge. And what they saw was enough to convince them that they were all completely crazy in the head. No sane person would have believed he was seeing right.

"Maybe it's what they call a mirage," Slam Dunk said, "when you see things that aren't there."

"Like camels," Dirk said.

"And palm trees," said Marvin.

"And horse tanks," said Little Harry.

They weren't seeing camels and palm trees, or horse tanks either, but rather the mighty forces—what was left of them—of Captain Girolamo K. Mayhem. Either they saw them or fancied they saw them. They weren't quite sure. And the music they were hearing—or fancied they were hearing—was the Bushmen's Hymn. It was coming from the loudspeaker atop the command post, where Captain Mayhem sat with Awful Ivan Hoffenhoff in two separate swivel chairs. Their arms were linked together in the spirit of comradeship, their chairs turning slowly beneath the blazing sun, while from the loudspeaker came the lilting strains of what sounded like a boys' choir singing *Waltzin' Through Sagebrush with You.*

It was a very touching scene—even, if you liked waltzes, inspiring. It was nice to see the old boys going mad so sweetly. Those grim old men, in their madness, were positively ecstatic. All along the trail, ahead and behind, the kickers and whackers, barely able to walk, were slowly— almost in slow motion—lifting their legs, to kick and whack the wilted bushes. They seemed so gentle, so considerate. Far in back of them, the wheels of the jeeps and patrol cars seemed to be spinning harmlessly in the sand. Everything had an air of being in a dream.

"Are you *sure* we're not delirious," Tiffany asked, "and imagining all this?"

"It's hard to tell," Charlie said. "The brain does do funny things when you're tired. But the dogs seem to think it's real."

"Dogs go crazy, too."

"Maybe we're just seein' what we want to see down there," Slam Dunk said.

"But that music is real," Marvin Lee said.

Waltzin' Through Sagebrush with You.

Far in the distance, beyond the Bushmen, something caught Charlie's eye. "Look over there," he told them, "toward the approach to Blanco Canyon. What do you see?"

They all looked, the dogs included. Charlie waited.

"It's the truck!" they all shouted together. "The Gone-Forever Mack!"

"We almost beat it to the canyon," Slam Dunk said.

"It probably broke down ten times," Marvin Lee said.

They watched as it disappeared up the canyon.

"They'll wait there," Slam Dunk said, "for stragglers."

"There's only one little catch," Charlie said. "We've got to go through Mayhem's Bushmen to get to the canyon. And they've got to go through us to get to the beeper, where they think we are. You might say we've got a problem on our hands."

"There's another little catch, too," Tiffany said, holding tightly to the dogs. "Somebody's standing right behind us."

They turned. And there he was, not four feet away. The Apache Stalker.

Cut off at the pass.

13

Slowly, very slowly, the Stalker's old musket came up. It seemed to take forever. To the disbelieving eyes of the fugitives, the gun moved, as everything seemed to move now, in slow motion. What they were seeing was real, but did not seem so. The Shock Factor, as Charlie might have called it, of seeing the Stalker had been too much for their tired minds. Now it was no longer a question of fact or fancy. It was simple disbelief. It couldn't be happening.

And yet, it was.

The musket rose, still slowly.

Then, very slowly also, Charlie said, "Wait!" not to the Stalker but to the disbelieving runners. He knew what state they were in. It was as if their lives were suspended, just hanging there. Hysteria would come next. Charlie also knew what state the Stalker was in. It was visible in his eyes. In a sense, his eyes weren't seeing anything. He was as close to being blind as you can get and still manage to see. But more importantly, he was as close to collapsing as you can get and still manage to stand.

"Wait," Charlie said again, softly. Then he went over very slowly to the Stalker, eased aside his gun, put his forefinger against his chest, and pushed ever so slightly. The Stalker sank to the ground.

"Poor old Ellsworth," Charlie said. "The desert got him."

That broke the spell. Everything was real again. Maybe, in their eyes, it was right again as well. They were back in their sunburned, waterless world, threatened only by the elements and the approaching Bushmen. The Shock Factor had crumbled. It lay at their feet, the object of the Afghans' curiosity.

"Is he blind?" Slam Dunk asked.

"Almost," Charlie said.

"Is he crazy in the head?" asked Little Harry.

"That for sure," said Charlie.

"What are we gonna do with him?" Tiffany asked.

"Bury him, of course," Little Harry said.

"Restore him," Charlie corrected. "He just needs a little attention."

"He needs a priest," Marvin Lee said.

"*I am a priest,*" the Stalker said, opening one eye to stare up at them.

"Holy Mother!" Tiffany cried.

"He's rising from the dead!" said Dirk the Turk.

"My time has come," the Stalker moaned. "Give me the holy water."

"All water is holy here," Charlie said. "You know that as well as I do, Ellsworth."

"Just a few drops on my lips," Ellsworth begged. "It might not save my soul, but it will do wonders for my body."

Dirty Little Harry was pitiless. "You bugged us," he said.

"That is a sin I must confess," Ellsworth said. "Now, about that water."

"You put Bugsy and Mugsy on us," Dirty Little Harry went on. "For money."

"Another sin," said Ellsworth. "I must also confess that I put the tax collector on you for the same reason." Ellsworth made a weak gesture. "He's back there somewhere dying of thirst."

"Are you really a priest?" Tiffany asked.

"A preacher," Ellsworth moaned. "Part-time. Now, the water."

They pulled him under some brush to keep the sun from finishing him. Far off in the distance, Captain Mayhem's choir was still singing, in parched, weak voices, *Waltzin' Through Sagebrush with You*. Though the voices were faint, they were steadily growing closer. High overhead, a few buzzards were beginning to circle. Goose One and Goose Two were nowhere to be seen.

Charlie went to work on Ellsworth, sacrificing a few drops of the precious water to moisten his lips. Then he laid a cloth over his eyes and left him in the shade. Ellsworth was still mumbling about the sins he had committed, promising never to repeat them. Charlie drew the troops aside.

"They're moving this way," Charlie said. "It's decision-making time."

"We know," they said.

They also knew that it was dying time, and going-crazy time. The desert was picking off victims at a rapid rate.

"You might call it do-or-die time," Charlie said.

"We know that, too."

"So," Charlie went on, "it's big stakes now—the whole pot, as poker players say. Either we win or we lose, cleanly, one way or the other. No regrets, no laments." He paused. They waited. Except for the panting of the dogs, and Ellsworth's moaning, the world around them was quiet. It was one of those moments when nobody has to say anything to be understood. After a while, Charlie said, "We've got one card left."

"One?" Marvin Lee asked in a small voice.

"One," Charlie said. "If we play it right, it's open road to Blanco Canyon. If we play it wrong, we may all look like Ellsworth there."

"No human should look like that," Tiffany said.

"We probably look worse," Dirty Little Harry said, "if we could see ourselves."

They did look pretty bad, but they were still on their feet. Still trying. Still plotting. Still hoping.

In the distance, the music grew closer. From the loudspeaker, you could hear Captain Mayhem's raspy voice crying out to his Bushmen to whack and kick everything in sight. "Flush 'em out!" they heard his weak voice faintly. Even more faintly came the voice of Awful Ivan crying, "Where are the windmills? Where are the horse tanks?"

"They're out of water, too," Charlie said. "Kind of evens things up."

"The casualty rate must be pretty high," Dirty Little Harry said.

"Never mind the casualty rate," Slam Dunk said. And then he asked the question that was in all their minds, "What's the card, Charlie?"

"Ellsworth," Charlie said. "He's our only hope."

"*Ellsworth!*" They were dumbfounded. Charlie had popped his cork.

"That's right," Charlie said. "He's all we've got. Our only card. The problem is, how to play it."

"We got one card left," Marvin Lee marveled. "That's Ellsworth. And we don't know how to play it." Yep, the heat had got Charlie.

"Let's play our card, then," Slam Dunk said, "and hope for the best."

"We better pray," Tiffany said, looking at the pitiful figure on the ground.

"Wouldn't hurt a thing," Charlie said. "I must confess— to use Ellsworth's word—that we're taking a terrible chance."

"What are we gonna do with him?" Marvin Lee asked. "Trade him for safe passage or something?"

"No," Charlie said. "They don't care about Ellsworth. In fact, they'd throw him to the coyotes if he didn't have any useful information. So we're gonna give him some useful information, something he can sell, and send him down the hill—hoping, of course, he doesn't die before he gets there. That would really complicate things. Here's what we do. We make him promise not to reveal our position, which means of course that he will reveal our position. Mayhem will send his forces straight at us, but we won't be here. We'll be over there"—Charlie pointed to the west— "on the old Comanche Trail."

"I think I'm beginning to see," Slam Dunk said. "But can we trust him—to be untrustworthy, I mean?"

"I'm bettin' our lives on it," Charlie said.

"You sure live dangerously," Slam Dunk said.

"It's a dangerous world," Charlie said. "There are some things you can count on and some things you can't. I'm countin' on Ellsworth to lie to us, even with his dying breath."

"I'm with Charlie," Dirty Little Harry said.

"I'm not so sure," Tiffany said. "He sounds real penitent. Maybe he's changed."

"Yeah," said Marvin Lee. "Like born again or something."

"Not a chance," said Charlie. "When it comes down to money, Ellsworth will sell us all out—no matter what he promises."

The song from the caravan grew closer. Mayhem and his Bushmen were now not more than half a mile away. They were moving steadily toward the fugitives and toward the beeper far behind them.

"How much water we got left?" Charlie asked.

They shook their canteens. Most made no noise at all. One or two had a few drops, and Charlie figured he had one good swig left—hot but good.

"We've got to sacrifice a few drops," he said, "to coax Ellsworth into action."

It didn't take long to get Ellsworth to his feet. The promise of water did it. To a dying man, there's nothing like the gurgly sound of a canteen. Ellsworth reached out. "I'll never forget you for this," he said.

"You haven't got it yet," Charlie said. "First, we make a pact."

"A sacred pact," said Marvin Lee.

"An unbreakable pact," said Dirk.

"Anything. Anything," Ellsworth moaned. "Just give me the water."

Charlie held the canteen in front of Ellsworth's face. "This will save your life," he said. "In exchange for the water, we want a favor from you. We're giving you a chance, maybe your last chance on this earth, to do something good. We're also giving you one last chance to choose between lying and telling us the truth."

Ellsworth began to slobber. Charlie was pressing him hard.

"Now, listen closely," Charlie said.

"I'm listening," Ellsworth moaned.

"We're giving you a little of our water. Then you are going down the hill to Captain Mayhem. You will not reveal our position to him. You will tell him nothing. Promise."

"I promise."

"If he asks you where we are," Charlie went on, "point west, toward the old Comanche Trail. God will forgive you for that little gesture. What's more, it'll save our lives."

"I promise," Ellsworth moaned, reaching for the water.

"You're not lying?"

"No."

"Swear it," Dirty Little Harry said.

"I swear it," Ellsworth groaned.

"Swear it on the Bible," Marvin Lee said.

"I haven't got a Bible," Ellsworth said. "But I will swear by all the angels and the saints and martyrs and my friends and relatives, good and bad, living and dead, and by all the sacred books in the El Paso Divinity School, where I first heard the Call."

"That's aplenty," Charlie said.

Then he gave him the water. It was not a pleasant sight to see him swill the few hot drops. He kept on trying after the water was gone. Finally, they had to tear the canteen from his mouth, lest he chew it to pieces.

Scary. Pitiful. Desert madness. Going-crazy time. Maybe dying time.

"Now," Charlie said, "let me look at you." He stood there looking straight at Ellsworth. It was as if he were looking at some poker player's face before deciding whether to play or fold the last card. He had to know what was in Ellsworth's twisted mind. He had to be sure. Their lives depended on it. Would he keep his promise? Was he lying? Was he bluffing? Would he still do anything for money? Finally he saw it, or thought he saw it. It was in Ellsworth's half-mad eyes.

"Go," he said.

Ellsworth started staggering down the hill. In a little while, he was lost from sight in the brush.

"I suppose you know," Tiffany said, "our lives are in his hands. That makes me nervous."

"Do you think he'll keep his word?" Slam Dunk asked.

"Not for a minute," Charlie said.

"Have you ever been wrong, Charlie?" Marvin Lee asked.

"Twice," said Charlie. "Both times when I was very tired."

"Are you very tired now?" Dirk asked.

"About the same as you," Charlie said.

"Then we're done for," Dirk replied.

"Let's move out," Charlie said. "Straight west. To the old Comanche Trail."

They weren't running now. In fact, they were almost crawling. It was the hottest time of the day. Even the lizards and rattlesnakes had taken cover. As they slowly made their way west, sneaking from bush to bush and rock to rock, in all their minds was the same question: Could they really rely on Ellsworth to be unreliable? It seemed so strange, as Tiffany had said, to put your life in the hands of someone so pitiful and confused. But there was nothing they could do about it now.

Actually, there wasn't even any time to think about it; for just as they reached the old Comanche Trail, Ellsworth drew in sight of Mayhem's command post. A shout went up from the captain, still swiveling in his chair alongside Awful Ivan. "It's the scout! It's the scout! Bring him in. Get him some water. Bring him up to me. Pour some water down him."

The captain was raving louder than ever now, partly from the anticipation of victory, and partly from the unrelenting sun. Beside him in the other swivel chair, Awful Ivan turned slowly about, a vacant look on his face. At his feet, Halfway Hebe lay in a heap.

"Give the scout some water," Mayhem ordered.

"We're out of water, sir," the faithful aide replied.

"Borrow some from Diehard Kammerlock," the captain shouted.

"Diehard Kammerlock is missing in action, sir," the aide shouted back. "It is presumed he died very hard."

"Never mind," Mayhem shouted. "Apaches don't need water, anyway. Push the scout up here."

Now Captain Mayhem's forces were less than a hundred yards away. You could see every gesture, hear every word. When they had pushed Ellsworth up to the command chair, Mayhem pulled a water jug from under a sack. Ellsworth grabbed it like a dying man, biting and chewing at the neck.

"Drink!" Mayhem ordered.

"There's nothing in it," Ellsworth protested.

The fugitives watched. "Let's hope he doesn't die on the spot," Slam Dunk said.

He didn't. He just kept gnawing at the empty jug while Captain Mayhem kept asking questions.

"Where are the aliens?" he asked Ellsworth. "Speak, man! Speak! Point 'em out!"

Ellsworth hesitated, looking dumbly at the empty water jug.

"Here comes the card," Charlie said. "Keep your eyes on Ellsworth."

But Ellsworth didn't point. Ellsworth just stood there. Maybe Ellsworth was too weak to point. Maybe Ellsworth had died standing up. Which made no difference to the raging captain. He knew that, dead or alive, Ellsworth could hear the sound of money.

So now the captain prepared to play *his* card. Getting on the loudspeaker, he began addressing the kickers and whackers, many of whom were stretched out on the ground where they had fallen. Dutifully they rose and assembled before the command post.

"Men," said Mayhem, "we've got the fugitives in a trap. Ellsworth the great Apache Stalker knows where they are. When he points out their position, I want you to converge on that spot. Understood?"

"Understood," said the Bushmen.

"Can we kick 'em around a little?" one Bushman asked.

"As you wish," the captain said.

"He looks like he'd do it, too," Slam Dunk said of the Bushman.

"Now," the captain said to Ellsworth, "I am offering you

a bonus—call it a reward—to point out the position of the aliens." The captain held up a handful of bills. "Hundreds," he said.

That did it. Slowly Ellsworth turned, lifted his right hand, and pointed straight to the fugitives' original position.

"He lied to us," said Tiffany.

"With his dying breath," said Dirk.

"*Attack!*" the captain roared. The troops converged. Dust followed them as they scrambled up the rocky slope, the captain's command post rumbling along behind.

"We played it right," Charlie said.

The final card had fallen. Now nothing stood between them
and Blanco Canyon.

For a moment, they didn't quite know how to take it.
They wanted to celebrate, but were too tired. They wanted
to brag, but were too tired for that, too. Bells should have
rung. Trumpets should have sounded. Someone should
have said something memorable. But none of that happened. The best they could come up with came from Dirk
the Turk, the up-and-down champion of the world. "Now
can we flop?" he grunted wearily.

"Flop," said Charlie.

They flopped. Dogs and all.

Flop. Nothing memorable. But the word did have a certain beauty about it. Made for the occasion. It fit. Said everything.

Charlie, however, didn't flop. Instead, he began to stretch his legs, loosen his muscles, and—most revealing of all to the surprised fugitives—brush his beard into its streamlined pattern. No wind resistance. No drag. The wind in his face.

"No, Charlie," Slam Dunk said quietly. "No."

Charlie honed his nose and popped his knees. Then he went to work on his toes.

"No, Charlie, no," Tiffany said.

Pop. That was Charlie's big toe.

"Don't do it, Charlie," Marvin Lee said.

Tarsus. Metatarsus. The twenty-six bones. Stretching and popping. Messages to the spine. Messages to the mind.

"He's gonna do it," said Dirk the Turk.

"Yeah," said Dirty Little Harry. "Just like the Wild Bunch. In a cloud of dust."

"Gather round," said Charlie, continuing his snaps and pops and snorts.

For a moment they just sat there, where they had flopped. But then, one by one, they pushed themselves up and joined in the ritual. Knees, toes, joints. Everything was popping.

"Just follow the old Comanche Trail," Charlie said, "straight into Blanco Canyon."

"You sure you can't come?" Tiffany tried one more time.

"It's your race now," Charlie said. "In fact, it always was. I was just the wild card."

"You made the difference," said Dirk.

"You gave us the edge," said Marvin.

"We beat them all," said Dirty Little Harry.

"There's just one thing," Charlie said. "Nobody will ever believe you if you tell them."

"We don't care," Tiffany said. "*We* know."

All of them were loosened up now. Still they kept on doing the swings and sways with their bodies, smoothing out whatever kinks might be lingering there. While they swung, Charlie divided up the few remaining drops of water, passing the canteens around the circle. While they swayed, all of them tightened up the straps on their Sweet Life Running Suits, adjusted the Arabian head shawls, and knotted their Bloomie Bags. They even continued to swing and sway and bend and snap and pop and run in place while putting their hands together in the circle and carrying out what might be called their Goodbye High. When the High had reached the point where even the dogs joined in, Charlie eased himself away from the group, made a little turn, began to circle, then swung wider around the edges of the rocks and started floating. Soon—rising, falling, floating—he was streaming southward toward the border.

Goodbye, Charlie.

Behind him, the fugitives, watched curiously by the Afghans, continued their jogging in place. Then they, too, swung out in a small circle, made one turn, and headed north. They were led by Dirk the Turk, who, though going mostly up and down, was in his heart convinced that he was streaming.